William George Puddefoot

The minute man on the frontier

William George Puddefoot

The minute man on the frontier

ISBN/EAN: 9783337148119

Printed in Europe, USA, Canada, Australia, Japan

Cover: Foto ©Andreas Hilbeck / pixelio.de

More available books at **www.hansebooks.com**

THE REV. W. G. PUDDEFOOT, A.M.

FIELD SECRETARY OF THE HOME MISSIONARY SOCIETY

NEW YORK: 46 East 14th Street

THOMAS Y. CROWELL & COMPANY

BOSTON: 100 Purchase Street

Typography by C. J. Peters & Son,
Boston.

PREFACE.

In a very able review of Maspero's "Dawn of Civilization," the writer says "that for hundreds of years it was believed that history had two eyes; but now we know she has at least three, and that archæology is the third."

This may account for the saying that "history is a lie agreed to;" for it needs to be argus-eyed to give us any adequate idea of the truth; and while the writer of the following sketches does not aspire to the rank of a historian, he has been induced to print them for two or three reasons. First, because urged to by friends; and secondly, because of the unique condition of American frontier

life that is so rapidly passing away for-
ever.

One may read Macaulay, Froude,
Knight, and, in fact, a half-dozen histories of England, and then sit down to
the gossipy sketches of Sidney culled
from Pepys's, Evelyn's, and other diaries,
and get a truer view of English life
than in all the great histories combined.
It would be impossible to give even the
slightest sketch of a country so large as
ours for a single decade in many vol-
umes; although, in one sense, we are
more homogeneous than many suppose.

There was a greater difference in two
counties in England before the advent
of the railways than between two of our
Northern States to-day. To-day a man
may travel from Boston to San Fran-
cisco, and he will find the same head-
lines in his morning papers, and for three
thousand miles will find the scenery

desecrated by the wretched quack medicine advertisements that produce " that tired feeling " which they profess to cure.

If he goes into one county in the mother country, he will find the people singeing the bristles of their swine, and counting by the score, in another by the stone, etc., and customs kept up that had grown settled before travel became general. But with us it is different. We had no time to become crystallized before the iron horse, the great cosmopolitan of the age, rapidly levelled all distinctions; and it is only by getting away from the railway, and into settlements that still retain all the primitiveness of an earlier day, that we find the conditions of which much of this book treats.

CONTENTS.

LIST OF ILLUSTRATIONS.

THE MINUTE-MAN

ON

THE FRONTIER.

———

I.

THE FRONTIER IN RELATION TO THE WORLD.

THE opening up of a new frontier is world-wide in its operations. Minnesota entered the Union as a State in 1858. The putting to practical use the Falls of St. Anthony was felt all over Europe. Thousands of little country mills, nestling amid the trees, and adding to the beauty of the English pastoral scenery, to-day stand idle, the great wheels covered with green moss; and Tennyson's "Miller" becomes a reminiscence. Iowa became a State in 1846, and now leads the world in the production of corn; and although it is a thousand miles from the seaboard, yet through its immense production, and with the cheapening of transportation, we find over seventy thousand Italians emmigrating to this country, as, in spite of low wages, they cannot compete on the plains of Lombardy. (See Wells's " Economic Changes.") — We find that the man at the front can ship from Chicago to Liverpool the product of five acres of grain for less money than the cost of manuring one acre of land in England. (*Ibid.*)

Every time a new frontier in America is opened, it means both prosperity and disaster. So large are the opportunities, so rich the results, that at first all calculations are upset. Natural gas in the Middle States changes the price of coal in Europe. The finding of a tin-mine is felt in Cornwall and Wales the next day. The opening of the iron-mines in Michigan makes Cornish towns spring up in the upper peninsula, while the finding of ore in desolate places has caused communities to spring up with all the conditions of a cosmopolitan civilization, and we have to-day men living twenty-five miles from trees or grass. But such is the energy of the frontier type, that grass-plats have been carried and planted on the solid rocks, as in Duluth, where hundreds of thousands of dollars are expended in the grading of streets, and the opening of the sewers, all having to be blasted to do the work.

North Dakota was a wilderness of 150,-000 square miles, and had not produced a single bushel of wheat for sale, in 1881. In 1886 it produced nearly 35,000,000 bushels; in 1887, 62,553.000. (See Wells's "Recent Economic Changes.") The opening up of these immense territories starts railways from California to Siberia; for, with the Great West competing. Russia is stirred to greater effort. India, with her great commerce with Great Britain, needs a shorter route; and the Suez canal is made. Australia must compete with the Western plains; and great steamers, filled with refrigerators, are constructed for carrying fresh beef. The South American republics respond in return.

The hardy pioneer, ever on the move, explores well nigh impracticable routes in search of precious metals. The inventive mechanic must respond with an engine that can climb anywhere; and in almost inaccessible mountain eyries the eagle is disturbed by the shriek of the locomotive, and the bighorn must take refuge with the bison in the National Park. The news of new mines flies around the world, fortunes are made and lost in a day, and the destinies of nations determined. A great crop starts railways, steamships. Miners, smelting-works, iron and steel, respond. Letters fly across the Atlantic, and returning steamers are filled with eager men and women, who answer the letters in person. Down from the far north, Sweden and Norway have responded with over a million of their children. Great Britain has sent nearly six millions. Germany follows with 4,417,950; Italy. 392,000; France. 315, 130; Austria, 304,976; Denmark, 114,

858 ; Hungary, 141,601 ; Switzerland, 167,-203 ; Russia and Poland, 326,994 ; Netherlands, 99,516 ; and so on : in all, a total for Europe in fifty years of over 13,000,-000, the great majority of whom have been started from their homes by the opening up of new frontiers.

It has been stated on good authority, that sixty per cent of the Germans that come are between the ages of fifteen and forty, while all Germany has only thirty per cent of that age.

On the authority of Dr. Farr, quoted by R. Mayo Smith in his " Emigration and Immigration," he calculates the money value of the immigrants from the British Isles from 1837 to 1876 reached the enormous sum of 1,400,000 pounds sterling, or 7,000,000,000 of dollars, an average of 175,000,000 dollars a year ; while the amount sent back from British North America and the United States since 1848 was but £32,294,596.   And what has been produced by the immigrant and exported amounts to many hundred millions of dollars. It has been computed that the country has been pushed forward a quarter of a century by this vast mass of immigrants, nearly all of whom labor for a living.

The frontiers of America will yet change the world. When in the not distant future hundreds of millions cover the great continent, dotted with schools and churches, and an intelligent population speaking one language, and with other millions in Africa, Australia, and the islands of the sea, using the same language, the time will come when they will arbitrate for the world, and war shall be no more. Long before the Atlantic cable was stretched across the ocean, millions of heartstrings were vibrating from this land to all parts of Europe; and to-day the letters fly homeward from the frontier immigrants in their sod houses, bearing good cheer in words and money.

The freedom of the frontier is contagious, and the poor European strives harder than ever to reach his kin across the sea. And when we consider that only 300,000 square miles out of 1,500,000 miles of arable land is under cultivation, and that already the farmers of England and most parts of Europe are being pushed to the wall, we begin to realize that the growth of the frontiers of the United States not only influences our own land, but changes materially the course of events in the whole world. The above figures are by Mr. Edward Atkinson, as quoted in substance from " Recent Economic Changes."

To show the growth of one State during the past fifty years, let us take Michigan. In 1840 Michigan had a population of 212,267 ; in 1890, 2,093,889. In 1840 there were three small railroads, with a total mileage of 59 miles. In 1890 there were over 7,000 miles. " In 1840 [I quote from Hon. B. W. Cutcheon, in " Fifty Years' Growth in Michigan "] mining had not begun. In 1890 over 7,000,000 tons of iron were shipped from her mines ; while the output of copper had reached

over a 100,000,000 lbs., and valued at
$15,845,427.28. The salt industry, a late
one, rose from 4,000 bbls. in 1860 to
3,838,937 bbls. in 1890; while the value
of her lumber products for 1890 was over
$55,000,000. In 1840 there were neither
graded nor high schools, normal schools
nor colleges. In 1890, 654,502 children
were of school age, with an enrolment of
427,032, with 33,975 additional attending
private schools. These children were
taught by 15,990 teachers, who received
in salaries $3,326,287."

In 1840 Michigan had 30,144 horses
and mules, 185,190 neat cattle, 99,618
sheep. In 1890 there were 579,896
horses, 3,779 mules, of milch cows 459,-
475, oxen and other cattle 508,938, of
sheep 2,353,779, of swine 893,037. The
total value came to $74,892,618. Over
1,700 men are engaged in the fisheries,
with nearly a million dollars invested,
with a total yield of all fish of 34,490,184
lbs., valued at over a million and a half
of dollars. The value of her apples and

peaches in 1890 was $944,332; of cherries, pears, and plums, $65,217; of straw-berries, $166,033; of other berries, $267,-398; and of grapes, $122,394. The wheat crop for 1891 was valued at $27,-486,910; the oats at $9,689,441; besides 811,977 bushels of buckwheat, and 2,522,-376 bushels of barley. The capital invested in lumber alone was $111,302,797. "While her great University, which saw its first student in 1841, and which had but three teachers, one of them acting as president, has grown to be one of the largest in the nation, with eighty professors and instructors and 2,700 students registered on her rolls, conferring 623 degrees upon examination." And all this but the partial record of fifty years in one State.

Since Michigan was entered as a State fourteen new States have been formed (not counting Texas) and three Territories, with an aggregate of over 17,000,000 square miles of land, and a population of nearly 15,000,000, nearly all of which fifty years ago was wilderness, the home of the Indian and the wild beasts. With such stupendous changes in so short a time, we see that the American fron tiers have a direct and powerful influence in changing the histories and destinies of the nations of the whole world.

II.

EARLY REMINISCENCES.

It was in the spring of 1859 that I first saw the frontier. Our way was over the New York Central, very little of which had two tracks. I have a very vivid recollection of the worm fences, the log houses, and the great forests that we passed on our way to Upper Canada. I remember the hunters coming towards the train with their moccasons on and the bucks slung over their shoulders. I have since that time seen many men who were the first to cut a tree in this county or that town. There were about forty thousand miles of railway in the whole land at that date, against nearly two hundred thousand miles to-day. Cities which are now the capitals of States were the feeding-ground of buffalo; wolves and black bears had their dens where to-day we can see a greater miracle in stone than Cheops; i.e., a stone State House built inside the appropriation! Then six miles of travel on the new roads smashed more china than three thousand miles by sea and rail. The little towns were but openings in a forest that extended for hundreds of miles. The best house in the village without a cellar; roots were kept in pits. Houses could be rented for two dollars per month, where to-day they are twelve dollars. Pork was two dollars a hundred; beef by the quarter, two and one-half cents a pound; potatoes, fifteen cents a bushel. Men received seventy-five cents a day for working on the railroad. Cord-wood was two dollars a cord; and you could get it cut, split, and piled for fifty cents a cord. Men wore stogy boots, generally with one leg of the trousers outside and one in. Blue denham was the prevailing suit for workingmen. The shoemaker cut his shoes, and they were sent out to be bound by women. The women wore spring-heeled shoes, print dresses, and huge sunbonnets; and in the summer-time the settlers went barefooted. The roads were simply indescribable. When a tree fell, it was cut off within an inch of the ruts; the wagon would sink to the hubs, and need prying out with poles; harnesses were never cleaned, and boot-blacking had no sale. But the school-house was in every township. In the older settlements could be seen the log hut in which the young couple started housekeeping, then a log house of more pretentious size; the frame-house which followed, and a fine brick house where the family now lived, showing the rapid progress made.

This was in western Canada. Toronto was separated from Yorkville, but was a busy, substantial city. I remember the stores being closed when Lincoln was buried, and black bunting hung along the principal streets. I remember, too, the men who were loudest in their curses at the government and against Lincoln, how the tears came to their eyes, and how that event brought them to their senses. Most of them were shoemakers from New England.

In 1873 I crossed into Michigan with my family. Even as late as that the greater part of northern Michigan, and especially the upper peninsula, was *terra incognita* to most of the people of that State. The railroads stopped at a long distance this side the Straits of Mackinaw. The lumbermen had but skimmed the best of the trees ; and, with the exception of a few isolated settlements on the lakes and up the larger rivers, it was an un-broken wilderness, abounding in fish, deer, bears, wolves, and wild-cats ; in fact, a hunter's paradise, as it is even to this day.

But with the extension of the railways to the Straits of Mackinaw, and the open-ing of new lines to the north into the iron mines of Menominee to the Gogebic range, the great copper mines of the Keweenaw peninsula, and the ever-increasing traffic of the lakes, the changes were simply marvellous. Some things I shall say will seem paradoxical, but they are nevertheless true to life.

The greater parts of southern Michigan and southern Wisconsin were settled by people from New York State ; and long before the northern parts of Michigan and Wisconsin were opened up, new States had risen in the West, and the tide of immigration swept past towards new frontiers, leaving vast frontiers behind them. Sometimes a few stray men with money at their command would pierce the country and form a settlement, as in the case of Traverse City. Here for years the mail was brought by the Indians on dog-sledges in the winter. It took eight days to reach Grand Rapids on snow-shoes. It is four hundred miles by water to Chicago. Sometimes the winters were so long that the provisions had to be dealt out very sparingly ; but all the time the little colony was growing, and when at last the railroads reached it, the traveller, after riding for miles through virgin forests, would come upon a little city of four thousand people, with good churches, fine schools, and one store that cost one hundred thousand dollars to build.

If it chanced to be summer-time he would see the tepees of the Indians along the bay, and two blocks back civilized homes with all the conveniences and luxuries of modern life. Here a huge canoe made of a single log, and there a mammoth steamer with all the elegances of an ocean-liner. Should he go on board of one of the steamers coasting around the lakes with supplies, he would pass great bays with lovely islands, and steam within a stone's throw of a comparatively rare bird, the great northern diver, and suddenly find himself near a wharf with a village in sight — a great saw-mill cutting its hundreds of thousands of feet of lumber a day; and near by, Indian graves with the food still fresh inside, and a tame deer with a collar and bell around its neck trotting around the streets.

INDIAN CAMP, GRAND TRAVERSE BAY, MICHIGAN.

Page 16.

He can sit and fish for trout on his doorstep that borders the little stream, or he can get on the company's locomotive and run twenty miles back into the woods and see the coveys of partridges rising in clouds, and here and there a timid doe and her fawn, whose curiosity is greater than their fears, until the whistle blows, and they are off like a shot into the deep forest, near where the black bear is munching raspberries in a ten-thousand-acre patch, while millions of bushels of whortleberries will waste for lack of pickers. He can sit on a point of an inland lake and catch minnows on one side, and pull up black bass on the other; and if a "tenderfoot" he will bring home as much as he can carry, expecting to be praised for his skill. He is mortified at the request to please bury them. He will ride over ground that less than fifteen years ago could be bought for a song and to-day produces millions, and is dotted with towns and huge furnaces glowing night and day.

If in the older settled parts, he will ride through cornfields whose tassels are up to the car windows, where the original settler paddled his skiff and caught pickerel and the ague at the same time, and who is still alive to tell the story. He can talk with a man who knew every white man by name when he first went there, and remembers the Indian peeping in through his log-cabin window, but whose grandchildren have graduated from a university with twenty-seven hundred students, where he helped build the log schoolhouse; who remembers when he had to send miles for salt, and yet was living over a bed of it big enough to salt the world down.

He had nothing but York State pumpkins and wild cranberries for his Thanksgiving dinner, with salt pork for turkey; and he lives to-day in one of the great fruit belts of the world, and ships his turkeys by the ton to the East; and to-day in the North the same experience is going on. Places where the mention of an apple makes the teeth water, and where you can still see them come wrapped in tissue paper like oranges, and yet, paradoxical as it may seem, you can enter a lumber-camp and find the men regaled on roast chicken and eating cucumbers before the seed is sown in that part of the country.

Here are farms worth over eighty thousand dollars, which but a few years ago were entered by the homesteader who had to live on potatoes and salt, and cut wild hay in summer, and draw it to town on a cedar jumper, in order to get flour for his hungry children. Here on an island are men living who used to leave their farming to see the one steamer unload and load, or watch a schooner drawn up over the Rapids, and who now see sweeping by their farms a procession of craft whose tonnage is greater than all the ocean ports of the country.

I have sat on the deck of a little steamer and drawn pictures for the Indians, who took them and marched off with the smile of a schoolboy getting a prize chromo, and in less than five years from that time I have at the same place sat down in a hotel lighted with electricity, and a menu equal to any in the country, with a bronze portrait of General Grant embossed on the top. Within ten years I have preached, with an Indian chief for an interpreter, in a log house in which a half-brother of Riel of North-Western fame was a hearer, where to-day there are self-supporting churches and flourishing schools.

Less than sixteen years ago I stopped at the end of the Michigan Central Railway, northern division ; every lot was filled with stumps. A school was being rapidly built, while the church had a lot only. The next time I visited the town it had fine churches and schools. The hotel had a beautiful conservatory filled with choice flowers. I could take my train, pass on over the Straits of Mackinaw, on by rail again, and clear to the Pacific, with sleeper and dining-car attached.

VIEW NEAR PETOSKEY, MICHIGAN.

But once leave your railway, and soon you can get to settlements twenty years old which saw the first buggy last year come into the clearings. Here are deep forests where the preacher on his way home from church meets the panther and the wild-cat, and where as yet he must ford the rivers and build his church, the first in nine thousand square miles.

III.

THE MINUTE-MAN ON THE FRONTIER.

THE minute-men at the front are the nation's cheapest policemen; and strange as it may seem, these men stand in vital relations to all the great cities of the country from which they are so far removed. It is a well-known fact that every city owes its life and increase to the fresh infusion of country blood, and it depends largely on the purity of that blood as to what the moral condition of the city shall be. Therefore it is of the utmost importance that Zion's watchmen shall lift up their voices day and night, until not only the wilderness shall be glad because of them, but that the city's walls may be named Salvation and her gates Praise.

Let us make the rounds among our minute-men to see how they live and what they do. Our road leads along the Grand

Rapids and Indiana Railway. All day long we have been flitting past new towns, and toward night we plunge into · the dense forests with only here and there an opening. The fresh perfume of the balsam invades the cars, the clear trout-streams pass and repass under the track, a herd of deer scurry yonder, and once we see a huge black bear swaying between two giant hemlocks.

At eleven P.M. we leave the train. There is a drizzling rain through which we see a half-dozen twinkling lights. As the train turns a curve we lose sight of its red lights, and feel we have lost our best.friend. A little boy, the sole human being in sight, is carrying a diminutive mail-bag. The sidewalk is only about thirty-six feet long. Then among the stumps we wind our slippery way, and at last reach the only frame house for miles. To the north and east we see a wilderness, with here and there a hardy settler's hut, sometimes a wagon with a cover and the stump of a stove-pipe sticking through the top.

After climbing the stairs, which are destitute of a balustrade, we enter our room. It is carpeted with a horse-blanket. Starting out with a lumber wagon next morning, with axes and whip-saw, we hew our way through the forest to another line of railway, and returning, are asked by the people in the settlement, " Will it ever be settled ? " " Could a man raise apples ? "   " Snow too deep ? "   " Mice girdle all the trees, eh ? " etc.

Five years later, on a sleeping-car, we open our eyes in the morning, and what a change! The little solitary stations that we passed before are surrounded with houses. White puffs of steam come snapping out from factories. A weekly paper, a New York and Boston store, and the five- and ten-cent counter store are among the developments. Our train sweeps onward, miles beyond our first stop ; and instead of the lonely lodging-house, palatial hotels invite us, bands of music are playing, the bay is a scene of magic, here a little naphtha launch, and there a steam yacht, and then a mighty steamer that makes the dock cringe its whole length as she slowly ties up to it.

Night comes on, but the woods are as light as day with electric lights. Rustic houses of artistic design are on every hand. Here, where it was thought apples could not be raised because of mice and deep snow, is a great Western Chautauqua.

Eighty thousand people are pushing forward into the northern counties of this great State. Roads, bridges, schoolhouses, — all are building. Most of the settlers are poor, sometimes having to leave part of their furniture to pay freight. They are from all quarters of our own and other lands. Here spring up great mill towns, mining towns, and county seats; and here, too, our minute-man comes. What can he do? Nearly all the people are here to make money. He has neither church, parsonage, nor a membership to start with. Here he finds towns with twenty saloons in a block, opera house and electric plants, dog-fights, men-fights, no Sabbath but an extra day for amusements and debauchery.

The minute-man is ready for any emergency; he takes chances that would appall a town minister. He finds a town without a single house that is a home; he has missed his train at a funeral. It is too cold to sleep in the woods, and so he walks the streets.

A saloon-keeper sees him. " Hello, Elder! Did ye miss yer train? Kind o' tough, eh?" with a laugh. " Well, ye ken sleep in the saloon if ye ken stand it." And so down on the floor he goes, comforting himself with the text, " Though I make my bed in hell, behold, thou art there."

Another minute-man in another part of the country finds a town given up to wickedness. He gets his frugal lunch in a saloon, the only place for him.

" Are you a preacher?"

" Yes."

" Thought so. You want to preach?"

" I don't know where I can get a hall."

" Oh, stranger, I'll give ye my dance-hall; jest the thing, and I tell ye we need preaching here bad."

" Good ; I will preach."

The saloon man stretches a large piece of cotton across his bar, and writes, —

" Divine service in this place from ten A. M. to twelve to-morrow. No drinks served during service."

It is a strange crowd: there are university men, and men who never saw a school. With some little trembling the minute-man begins, and as he speaks he feels ·more freedom and courage. At the conclusion the host seizes his big hat, and with a revolver commences to take up a collection, remarking that they had had some pretty straight slugging. On the back seats are a number of what are called five-cent-ante men ; and as they drop in small coin, he says, —

" Come, boys, ye have got to straddle that."

He brings the hat to the parson, and empties a large collection on the table.

"But what can I do with these colored things?"

"Why, pard, them's chips; every one redeemable at the bar in gold."

Sometimes the minute-man has a harder time. A scholarly man who now holds a high position in New England was a short time since in a mountain town where he preached in the morning to a few people in an empty saloon, and announced that there would be service in the same place in the evening. But he reckoned without his host. By evening it was a saloon again in full blast. Nothing daunted, he began outside.

The men lighted a tar-barrel, and began to raffle off a mule. Just then a noted bravo of the camps came down; and quick as a flash his shooting-irons were out, and with a voice like a lion he said, —

"Boys, I drop the first one that interferes with this service."

Thus under guard from unexpected quarters, the preacher spoke to a number of men who had been former church-members in the far East.

Often these minute-men must build their own houses, and live in such a rough society that wife and children must stay behind for some years. One minute-man built a little hut the roof of which was shingled with oyster-cans. His room was so small that he could pour out his coffee at the table, and without getting up turn his flapjacks on the stove. A travelling missionary visiting him, asked him where he slept. He opened a little trap-door in the ceiling; and as the good woman peered in she said, —

"Why, you can't stand up in that place!"

"Bless your soul, madam," he exclaimed, "a home missionary doesn't sleep standing up."

Strapping a bundle of books on his shoulders, this minute-man starts out on a mule-trail. If he meets the train, he must step off and climb back. He reaches the distant camp, and finds the boys by the dozen gambling in an immense saloon. He steps up to the bar and requests the liberty of singing a few hymns. The man answers surlily, —

"Ye ken if ye like, but the boys won't stand it."

The next minute a rich baritone begins, "What a friend we have in Jesus," and twenty heads are lifted. He then says, —

"Boys, take a hand; here are some books." And in less than ten minutes he has a male choir of many voices. One says, "Pard, sing number so and so;" and another, "Sing number so and so." By this time the saloon-keeper is growling; but it is of no use; the minister has the boys, and starts his work.

In some camps a very different reception awaits him, as, for instance, the following: At his appearance a wild-looking Buffalo-Bill type of man greeted him with an oath and a pistol levelled at him.

"Don't yer know thar's no luck in camp with a preacher? We are going to kill ye."

"Don't you know," said the minute-man, "a minister can draw a bead as quick as any man?" The boys gave a loud laugh, for they love grit, and the rough slunk away. But a harder trial followed.

"Glad to see ye, pard; but ye'll have to set 'em up 'fore ye commence — rule of the camp, ye know." But before our man could frame an answer, the hardest drinker in the crowd said, —

"Boys, he is the fust minister as has had the sand to come up here, and I'll stand treat for him."

It is a great pleasure to add that the man who did this is to-day a Christian.

One man is found on our grand round, living with a wife and a large family in a church. The church building had been too cold to worship in, and so they gave it to him for a parsonage. The man had his study in the belfry, and had to tack a carpet up to keep his papers from blowing into the lake. This man's life was in constant jeopardy, and he always carried two large revolvers. He had been the cause of breaking up the stockade dens of the town, and ruffians were hired to kill him. He seemed to wear a charmed life — but then, he was over six feet high, and weighed more than two hundred pounds. Some of the facts that this man could narrate are unreportable.

The lives lost on our frontiers to-day through sin in all its forms are legion, and no man realizes as well as the home missionary what it costs to build a new country; on the other hand, no man has such an opportunity to see the growth of the kingdom.

There died in Beloit, recently, the Rev. Jeremiah Porter, a man who had been a home missionary. His field was at Fort Brady before Chicago had its name. His church was largely composed of soldiers; and when the men were ordered to Fort Dearborn, he went with them, and organized what is now known as the First Presbyterian Church of Chicago. This minute-man lived to see Chicago one million two hundred thousand strong.

We should have lost the whole Pacific slope but for our minute-man, the glorious and heroic Whitman, who not only carried his wagon over the Rockies, but came back through stern winter and past hostile savages, and by hard reasoning with Webster and others secured that vast possession for us. As a nation we owe a debt we can never repay to the soldiers of the cross at the front, who have endured (and endure to-day) hardships of every kind. They are cut off from the society which they love; often they live in dugouts, sometimes in rooms over a saloon; going weeks without fresh meat, sometimes suffering from hunger, and for a long time without a cent in the house. Yet who ever heard them complain? Their great grief is that fields lie near to them white for the harvest, while, with hands already full, they can only pray the Lord of the harvest to send forth more laborers.

Often there is but one man preaching in a county which is larger than Massachusetts. He is cut off from libraries, ministers' meetings, and to a large extent from the sympathies of more fortunate brethren, and is often unable to send his children to college. These men still stand their ground until they die, ofttimes unknown, but leaving foundations for others to build on.

One place visited by a general missionary was so full of reckless men that the station-agent always carried a revolver from his house to the railway station. A vile variety show, carried on by abandoned women, was kept open day and night. Sunday was the noisiest day of all. Yet in this place a church was formed; and many men and women, having found a leader, were ready to take a stand for the right.

I am not writing of the past; for all the conditions that I have spoken of exist in hundreds, yes, thousands, of places all over the land. One need not go to the far West to find them; they exist in every State of the Union, only varying in their types of sin.

Visiting a home missionary in a mining region within two hours' ride of the capital, in a State not four hundred miles from the Atlantic, I found the man in one of the most desolate towns I ever saw. The most prosperous families were earning on an average five dollars a week, store pay. All were in debt. When the missionary announced his intention of going there, he was warned that it was not safe; but that did not alter his plans.

The first service was held in a school-house, the door panels of which were out and not a pane of glass unbroken. A roaring torrent had to· be passed on an unsteady plank bridge, over which the women and children crawled on hands and knees. It was dark when they came. The preacher could see the gleam of the men's eyes from their grimy faces as the lanterns flickered in the draughts. He began to preach. Soon white streaks were on the men's cheeks, as tears from eyes unused to weeping rolled down those black faces. At the close a church was organized, a reading-room was added, and many a boy was saved from the saloon by it. Yet, strange to say, although the owners (church members too) had cleared a million out of those mines, the money to build the needed church and parsonage had to be sent from the extreme East.

Hundreds of miles eastward I have found men living, sixty and seventy in number, in a long hut, their food cooked in a great pot, out of which they dipped their meals with a tin dipper. No less than seventy-five thousand Slovaks live in this one State, and their only spiritual counsel comes from a few Bible-readers. Ought we not then, as Christians, to help those already there, and give of our plenty to send the men needed to carry the light to thousands of places that as yet sit in the darkness and the shadow?

HOW THE HOME MISSIONARY BEGINS WORK IN THE NEW COMMUNITY.

First, pastoral visiting is absolutely necessary to success. The feelings of new-comers are tender after breaking the home ties and getting to the new home, and a visit from the pastor is sure to bring satisfactory results. Sickness and death offer him opportunities for doing much good, especially among the poor, and they are always the most numerous.

Some very pathetic cases come under every missionary's observation. Once a man called at the parsonage and asked for the elder, saying that a man had been killed some miles away in the woods, and the family wanted the missionary to preach the funeral sermon. The next morning a ragged boy came to pilot the minister. The way led through virgin forests and black-ash swamps. A light snow covered the ground and made travelling difficult, as much of the way was blocked by fallen trees. After two hours' walking the house was reached ; and here was the widow with her large family, most of them in borrowed clothes, the supervisor, a few rough men, and a county coffin.

The minister hardly knew what to say ; but remembering that that morning a large box had been sent containing a number of useful articles, he made God's providence his theme. A few days after, the box was taken to the widow's home. When they reached the shanty they found two little bunks inside. Her only stove was an oven taken from an old-fashioned cook-stove. The oven stood on a dry-goods box.

The missionary said, " Why, my poor woman, you will freeze with this wretched fire."

" No," she said ; " it ain't much for cooking and washing, but it's a *good* little heater."

A few white beans and small potatoes were all her store, with winter coming on apace. When she saw the good things for eating and wearing that had been brought to her, she sobbed out her thanks.

In the busy life of a missionary the event was soon forgotten, until one day a woman said, " Elder, do you recollect that 'ar Mrs. Sisco?"

"Yes."

" She is down with a fever, and so are her children."

At this news the minister started with the doctor to see her. As they neared the place he noticed some red streaks gleaming in the woods, and asked what they were.

" Oh," said the doctor, " that is from the widow's house. She had to move into a stable of the deserted lumber camp."

The chinks had fallen out from the

logs, and hence the gleam of fire. The house was a study in shadows — the floor sticky with mud brought in with the snow; the *débris* of a dozen meals on the table; a lamp, without chimney or bottom, stuck into an old tomato-can, gave its flickering light, and revealed the poor woman, with nothing to shield her from the storm but a few paper flour-sacks tacked back of the bed. Two or three chairs, the children in the other bed, the baby in a little soap-box on rockers, were all the wretched hovel contained. Medicine was left her, and the minister's watch for her to time it. He exchanged his watch for a clock the next day. By great persuasion the proper authorities were made to put her in the poorhouse, and she was lost to sight; but there was a bright ending in her case.

About a year after, a rosy-faced woman called at the parsonage. The pastor said, " Come in and have some dinner."

" I got some one waiting," she said.

" Why, who is that?"

" My new man."

" What, you married again ? "

" Yes ; and we are just going after
the rest of the traps up at the shanty, and
I called to see whether you would give me
the little clock for a keepsake ? "

" Oh, yes."

Away she went as happy as a lark.
Less than two years from the time she was
left a widow, a rich old uncle found in her
his long-lost niece, and the woman became
heiress to thousands of dollars.

Sometimes dreadful scenes are wit-
nessed at funerals where strong drink has
suddenly finished the career of father or
mother. At the funeral of a little child
smothered by a drunken father, the
mother was too sick to be up at the funeral, the father too drunk to realize what
was taking place, and twice the service
was stopped by drunken men. At another funeral a dog-fight began under the
coffin. The missionary kicked the dogs
out, and resumed as well as he could.

At another wretched home the woman
was found dying, the husband drunk, no

food, mercury ten degrees below zero, and the little children nearly perishing with cold. The drunken man pulled the bed from under his dying wife while he went to sleep. His awakening was terrible, and the house crowded at the funeral with morbid hearers.

In one town visited, a county town at that, the roughs had buried a man alive, leaving his head above ground, and then preached a mock funeral sermon, remarking as they left him, " How natural he looks ! "

As the nearest minister is miles away, the missionary has to travel many miles in all weathers to the dying and dead. Visiting the sick, and sitting up with those with dangerous diseases, soon cause the worst of men not only to respect but to love the missionary ; and no man has the moulding of a community so much in his hands as the courageous and faithful servant of Christ. The first missionary on the field leaves his stamp indelibly fixed on the new village. Towns left without the gospel for years are the hardest of all places in which to get a footing. Some towns have been without service of any kind for years, and some of the young men and women have never seen a minister. There are townships to-day, even in New York State, without a church; and, strange as it may seem, there are more churchless communities in Illinois than in any other State in the Union. Until two years ago Black Rock, with a population of five thousand, had no church or Sunday-school. Meanwhile such is the condition of the Home Missionary Society's treasury that they often cannot take the students who offer themselves, and the churchless places increase.

All kinds of people crowd to the front, — those who are stranded, those who are trying to hide from justice, men speculating. Gambling dens are open day and night, Sundays of course included, the men running them being relieved as regularly as guards in the army.

In purely agricultural districts a different type is met with. Many are so poor that the men have to go to the lumber woods part of the year. The women thus left often become despondent, and a very large per cent in the insane asylum comes from this class.

One family lived so far from town that when the husband died they were obliged to make his coffin, and utilized two flour-barrels for the purpose.

So amid all sorts and conditions of men, and under a variety of circumstances, the minute-man lives, works, and dies, too often forgotten and unsung, but remembered in the Book; and when God shall make up his jewels, some of the brightest gems will be found among the pioneers who carried the ark into the wilderness in advance of the roads, breaking through the forest guided by the surveyor's blaze on the trees.

There are hundreds of people who pierce into the heart of the country by going up the rivers before a path has been made. In one home found there, the minute-man had the bed in a big room down-stairs, while the man, with his wife and nine children, went up steps like a stable-ladder, and slept on " shakedowns," on a floor supported with four rafters which threatened to come down. But the minute-man, too tired to care, slept the sleep of the just. Often not so fortunate as then, he finds a large family and but one room. Once he missed his way, and had to crawl into two empty barrels with the ends knocked out. Drawing them as close together as he could, to prevent draughts, he had a short sleep, and awoke at four A.M. to find that a house and bed were but twenty rods farther.

In a new village, for the first visit all kinds of plans are made to draw the people out. Here is one : The minute-man calls at the school, and asks leave to draw on the blackboard. Teacher and scholars are delighted. After entertaining them for a while, he says, " Children, tell your parents that the man who chalk-talked to you will preach here at eight o'clock."

And the youngsters, expecting another such good time as they have just enjoyed, come out in force, bringing both parents with them. The village is but two years old. At first the people had the drinking-water brought five miles in barrels on the railroad, and for washing melted the snow. Then they took maple sap, and at last birch sap; but, "Law," said a woman, "it was dreadful ironin'!"

Here was a genuine pioneer: his house of logs, hinges wood, latch ditto, locks none; a black bear, three squirrels, a turtle-dove, two dogs, and a coon made up his earthly possessions. He was tired of the place.

"Laws, Elder! when I fust come ye could kill a deer close by, and ketch a string of trout off the doorsteps; but everything's sp'iled. Men beginning to wear b'iled shirts, and I can't stand it. I shall clear as soon as I can git out. Don't want to buy that b'ar, do ye?"

In this little town a grand minute-man laid down his life. He was so anxious to

A TYPICAL LOG HOUSE.

Page 46.

get the church paid for, that he would not buy an overcoat. Through the hard winter he often fought a temperature forty degrees below zero ; but at last a severe cold ended in his death. His good wife sold her wedding-gown to buy an overcoat, but all too late ; and a bride of a twelvemonth went out a widow with an orphan in her arms.

Yet the children of God are said to add to their already large store four hundred million dollars yearly, and some think of building a ten-million-dollar temple to honor God — while temples of the Holy Ghost are too often left to fall, through utter neglect, because we withhold the little that would save them. We shall never conquer the heathen world for Christ until we have learned the way to save America. Save America, and we can save the world.

IV.

THE IMMIGRANT ON THE FRONTIER.

WHATEVER may be the effect of immigrants in cities, the immigrant on the frontier has sent the country ahead a quarter of a century. In the first place, the pioneer immigrants are in the prime of life. They generally bring enough money to make a start. They need houses, tools, horses, and all the things needful to start. They seldom fail. Used to privation at home, they make very hardy settlers. In some States they comprise seventy per cent of the voters; and the getting of a piece of land they can call their own makes good citizens of them sooner than any other way. You can't make a dangerous kind of a man of him who can call a quarter section his own.

In order to show how the pioneer settler

from Europe prospers, let us begin with him at the wharf. There floats the leviathan that has a whole villageful on board, — over twelve hundred. They are on deck; and a motley crowd they appear, for they are from all lands. Here is a girl dressed in the picturesque costume of Western Europe, and here a man with a great peak to his hat, an enormous long coat, his beard half way down his breast, a china pipe as big as a small teacup in his mouth, his wife like a bundle of meal tied in the middle, with immense earrings, and an old colored handkerchief over her head. Behind them a half-dozen little ones with tow-heads of hair, looking as shaggy as Yorkshire terriers, blue-eyed and healthy. They are carrying copper coffee-pots and kettles; and away they march, eight hundred of them and more, up Broadway.

Here and there a man steps into a bakery, and comes out with a yard of bread, and breaks it up into hunks; and the little children grind it down without butter, with teeth that are clean from lack of meat, with all the gusto of Sunday-school children with angel-cake at a picnic. They are soon locked in the cars, and night comes on. Go inside and you will see the good mother slicing up bolognas or a Westphalia ham, and handing around slices of black bread. After supper reading of the Bible and prayers; and then the little ones are put into sack-like night-gowns, and put up in the top bunks, where they lie, watching their elders playing cards, until they fall asleep.

In the morning you go up to one of the women who is washing a boy and ask, as you see the great number of children around her, whether they are all hers: she courtesies and says, "Me no spik Inglish;" but by pantomime you make her understand, and she laughingly says, "Yah, yah;" and you think of Russell's song,—

"To the West, to the West, to the land of the free,
Where Mighty Missouri rolls down to the sea;
Where a man is a man, if he's willing to toil,
And the humblest may gather the fruits of the soil.

Where children are blessings, and he who has most,
Has aid for his fortune, and riches to boast;
Where the young may exult and the aged may rest—
Away, far away, to the land of the West!"

Their train is a slow one; it is side-tracked for the great fliers as they reach a single-track road.

The very cattle-trains have precedence of them. We watch their train as it reaches the great brown prairie; a little black shack or two is all you can see. The very tumble-weeds outstrip their slow-moving train; but after many weary hours they reach the end of the road, so far as it is built that day; it will go three miles farther to-morrow. As yet there are no freight-sheds, and they camp out on the prairie. The cold stars come out, the coyotes' sharp bark is heard in the distance, blended with the howl of the prairie wolf. Some of them dig holes in the side-hill, and put their little ones in them for the night. Tears come into the eyes of the mothers as they think of home and relatives beyond the seas.

And there we will leave them for twelve years, and then on one of our transcontinental palaces on wheels we will follow the immigrant trail. Where they passed black ash-swamps and marshes and scattered homes, we go through villages with public libraries; where they touched the brown prairie, we view a sea of living green; where they took five days, we go in two; where they stepped off at the end of the road, we stop at a junction whose steel rails run on to the Pacific or the Gulf of Mexico; where they made the shelter for their little ones in the ground, we find a good hotel, a city alive to the finger-tips, electric cars on the streets, an opera-house, and a high school just about to keep its commencement. On the street we notice some people that appear somewhat familiar, but we are not sure. When we spoke to them twelve years ago they said with a courtesy, " Me no spik Inglish;" but now without a courtesy they talk in broken English. The man has lost his big beard, his clothes are well-made; the wife is no longer like a bag of meal with a string around it. No; with a daily hint from Paris, she has all the feathers the law allows.

They are making for the high school-house, and we follow them. A chorus of fifty voices, with a grand piano accompaniment, is in progress as we take our seats, after which a boy stands forth and declaims his piece. We should never know him. It is one of our tow-headed youngsters from the wharf. The old father sits with tears of joy running down his wrinkled face. He can hardly believe his senses. He remembers when his grandsire was a serf under Nicholas, and it seems too good to be true. But he hears the neighing of his percherons under the little church-shed; and by association of ideas his fields and waving grain, his flocks, herds, and quarter section, rise before his mind's view, and he opens his eyes to see his favorite daughter step on the platform dressed in white, and great June roses drooping on her breast; and the old man's eyes sparkle as his daughter steps down amid a round of applause as she says in the very spirit of old Cromwell, " Curfew shall not ring to-night."

And this is real. It has been going on for a quarter of a century. States with whole counties filled with Russians voting, and being the banner counties to have prohibition in the State's Constitution ; or, like North Dakota, with nearly seventy per cent foreign voters, driving the lottery from them when needing money sorely. Men and women who could scarcely speak the English language living to see their sons senators and governors.

All the dismal prophecies about ruin from the immigrant are disproved as one looks over Wisconsin, Minnesota, and the Dakotas to-day ; and instead of having a great German nation on this side of the Atlantic, as one writer predicted, we have in the great agricultural States some of our stanchest American citizens.

One of the mightiest factors in human

life to-day is the language we use. Three centuries ago there were about 6,000,000 using it; to-day 125,000,000 speak the English tongue. The Duke of Argyle was once asked which was the best language. He said, " If I want to be polite I use the French, if I want to be understood I take the English, if I want to praise my Maker I take the Gaelic, my mother-tongue." Foreigners coming here think in their own language, even though they may be able to speak in ours; gradually they come to think in English, but still they dream in their mother-tongue; at last they dream, think, and speak in the language of the land, and become homogeneous with the nation.

God's greatest gift to this New World is the foreigner. The thought came to me while on my way to Savannah: Why did not the discoverers of the Western Hemisphere find a higher civilization than the one they left ? Why should God have kept so large a portion of the world hidden from the eyes of Europe for thousands of years? Had he not some grand design that in the fulness of time he would lead Columbus, like Abraham of old, to found a new nation?

Take your map and find those States which the stream of immigration has passed by, and in every case you find them behind the times. Strange how prejudice warps our vision! Jefferson said, " Would to God the Atlantic were a sea of flame;" and Washington said, "I would we were well rid of them, except Lafayette." Strange words for a man who would not have been an American had his ancestors not been immigrants. Hamilton, the great statesman, was an immigrant. Albert Gallatin the financier, Agassiz the scientist, and thousands of illustrious names, make a strong list. One-twelfth of the land foreigners! — but one-fourth of the Union armies were foreigners too.

WHAT THEY BECOME.

When Linnæus was under gardener, the head gardener had a flower he could not raise. He gave it to Linnæus, who took it to the back of a pine, placed broken ice around it, and gave it a northern exposure. In a few days the king with delight asked for the name of the beautiful gem. It was the Forsaken Flower.

So there are millions of our fellow-men in Europe to-day, in a harsh environment, sickly, poor, and ready to die; but when they are transplanted, they find a new home, clothes, food, and, above all, the freedom that makes our land the very paradise for the poor of all lands. These immigrants have made the brown prairie to blossom as the rose, the wilderness to become like the garden of the Lord. They drove the Louisiana Lottery out of North Dakota; they voted for temperance in South Dakota. Their hearts beat warm for their native land, but they are true to their adopted country.

The mixture of the nationalities is the very thing that makes us foremost: it has produced a new type; and if we but do our duty we shall be the arbitrator of the nations. There is no way to lift Europe so fast as to evangelize her sons who come to us. Sixteen per cent go home to live, and these can never forget what they saw here; did we but teach them aright, they would be an army of foreign missionaries, fifty thousand strong, preachers of the gospel to the people in the tongue in which they were born, and thus creating a perpetual Pentecost.

One other great fact needs pointing out. The discovery of this land was by the Latin races; and yet they failed to hold it, lacking the genius for colonization for which the Anglo-Saxon is pre-eminent. During the last fifty years, over 13,000,-000 immigrants have come to this land. Great Britain sent nearly 6,000,000; Germany, 4,500,000; Norway and Sweden, 939,603; Denmark, 144,858; the Netherlands, 99,522; Belgium, 42,102. Here we have over 11,000,000 Anglo-Saxon, Teutonic, and Scandinavian, of the 13,000,000, and almost half of them speaking English, while Italy, Russia, Poland, France, Austria, Switzerland, Hungary, Spain, Portugal, and all other nations sent but 1,708,897 out of the 13,296,157. And we must note also that nearly all of the Latin races came within the last few years; so that we were a nation 50,000,000 strong before many of them came, and eighty per cent of all our people speak English.

No nation ever drove out its people without loss, as witness Spain and France with their Protestants and Huguenots. England took them, and they helped to make her great. Often when a nation has actually been conquered in war, she in turn conquers her victors and is made better. Germany conquered Rome; but Roman laws and Roman government conquered the invaders, and made Germany the mother of modern civilization. Norsemen, Danes, and Saxons invaded Britain, and drenched her fields in blood. The Normans brought their beef, their mutton, and their pork, but the English kept their oxen, sheep, and swine; and eventually from the Norman, Dane, and others came the Anglo-Saxon race. England has four times as much inventive genius as the rest of Europe, but America has ten times as much as England; and why? Because added to the English colony is all Europe; and in our own people we have the practical Englishman, the thoughtful German, the metaphysical Scot, the quick-witted Irishman, the sprightly Gaul, the musical and artistic Italian, the hardy Swiss, the frugal and clear-headed Swede and Norwegian; and all united make the type which the world will yet come to, the manhood which will recognize the inherent nobility of the race, its brotherhood, and the great God, Father.

A TYPICAL SOD HOUSE.

V.

THE ODDITIES OF THE FRONTIER.

As the waves of the sea cast up all sorts of things, so the waves of humanity that flood the frontiers cast up all sorts and conditions of men. To go into a sod house and find a theological library belonging to the early part of the century, or to hear coming up through the ground a composition by Beethoven played on a piano, is a startling experience; so are some of the questions and assertions that one hears in a frontier Sunday-school.

I remember one old man who was in class when we were studying that part of the Acts of the Apostles where the disciples said, "It is not reason that we should leave the word of God and serve tables;" the old fellow said, "I have an idee that them tables was the two tables of stone that Moses brought down from the Mount." This was a stunner. I thought afterwards that the old man had an idea that they were to leave the law and stick to the gospel; but still it did not seem right to pick out men to serve the tables if that was what he meant.

Another would be satisfied with nothing but the literal meaning of everything he read. So when I explained to the class the modern idea of the Red Sea being driven by the wind so as to leave a road for light-laden people to walk over, the old man was up in arms at once, " Why," said he, " it says a wall ; " and no doubt the pictures which he had seen in his youth, of the children of Israel walking with bottle-green waters straight as two walls on either side, and the reading of a celebrated preacher's sermon, where it spoke of the fish coming up to peep at the little children, as if they would like a nibble, confirmed the old man in his views.

In vain I told him that a wind that would hold up such a vast mass of water would blow the Israelites out of their clothes ; still he stuck to his position until I asked him whether, when Nabal's men told him that David's men had been a wall unto them day and night, he thought that David had plastered them together ?

He said, " No ; it meant a defence," and apparently gave in, but muttered, " It says a wall, anyway."

Another man told me that if a man cut himself in the woods, there was a verse in the Bible so that if he turned to it and put his finger upon it, the blood would at once stop running ; and he wanted to know whether I knew where to find it. I told him I was very sorry that I did not know.

On the other hand, you may find a man with a Greek Testament, and well up in Greek, making his comments from the original. Here a Barclay & Perkins brewer from London, who has plunged into the woods to get rid of drink, and succeeded. Here a family, one of whom was Dr. Norman McLeod's nurse, and a playmate of the family. Another informs you he preached twenty-five years, "till his voice give out;" and here a Hard-shell Baptist, who "don't believe in Sunday-schools nohow."

The minute-man at the front needs to be ready for all emergencies, for he meets all kinds of original characters. One of the most successful men I ever heard of was the famous Father Paxton described by the Rev. E. P. Powell in the *Christian Register* in a very bright article from which I quote : —

When "blue," I always went down to the Depository, and begged him for a few stories. He rode a splendid horse, that was in full sympathy with his master, and bore the significant name, Robert Raikes. There were few houses except those built of logs. and these were not prejudiced against good ventilation. He laughed long and loud at his experience in one of these, which he reached one night in a furious storm. He was welcomed to the best, which was a single rude bed, while the family slept on the floor, behind a sheet hung up for that special occasion. Paxton was so thoroughly tired that he slept sound as soon as he touched the bed; but he half waked in the morning with the barking of a dog. The master of the house was shaking him, and halloing, " I say, stranger ! pull in your feet or Bowser 'll bite 'em ! " Stretching out in the night, he had run his feet through the side of the house, between the logs; and the dog outside had gone for them. The time he took in pulling in was so trifling as to be hardly worth the mention.

Those who know little of frontier life can have no idea of the difficulties to be met by a man with Paxton's mission. There was one district, not far from Cairo, that was ruled by a pious old fellow who swore that no Sunday-school should be set up "in that kidntry." Some one cautioned " the missioner " to keep away from M——, who would surely be as good as his word and thrash him. M—— was a Hard-shell Baptist, and owned the church, which was built also of logs. He lived in the only white-washed log house of the region. Instead of avoiding him, Father Paxton rode up one day, and jumping off Robert Raikes, hitched him to the rail that always was to be found before a Southern house. Old M —— sat straddle of a log in front of his door eating peaches from a basket. Paxton straddled the log on the other side of the basket, and helped himself. This was Southern style. You were welcome to help yourself so long as there was anything to eat. The conversation that started up was rather wary, for M—— suspected who his visitor was. Pretty soon Paxton noticed some hogs in a lot near them. "Mighty fine lot of hogs, stranger ! "

"And you mought say well they be a mighty fine lot of hogs."

"How many mought there be, stranger?"

"There mought be sixty-two hogs in that there lot, and they can't be beat."

Just then a little boy went up and grabbed a peach.

"Mought that be your young un, stranger?" asked Paxton.

"As nigh as one can say, that mought be mine."

"And a fine chap he be, surely."

"A purty fine one, I reckon myself."

"How many young ones mought you have, my friend?"

"Well, stranger, that's where you have me. Sally, I say, come to the door there! You count them childer while I name 'em — no, you name 'em, and I'll count."

So they counted out seventeen children. Paxton had his cue now, and was ready.

"Stranger, I say," he said, "this seems to me a curious kind of a kidntry."

"Why so, stranger?"

"Because, when I axed ye how many hogs ye had, ye could tell me plum off; but when I axed ye how many children ye had, ye had to count right smart before ye could tell. Seems to me ye pay a lettle more attention to your hogs than ye do to your childer."

"Stranger," shouted M——, "ye mought sure be the missioner. You've got me, sure! You shall have the church in the holler next Sunday, and me and my wife and my seventeen shall all be there."

True to his word, he helped Paxton to establish a school. When I was in St. Louis, there was a Sunday-school convention there. A fine-looking young man came up to Father Paxton, who was then in charge of the Sunday-school Depository, and said, —

" Don't ye know me, Father Paxton ? "

" No," said Paxton ; " I reckon I don't recall ye."

" Well, I am from ——; and I am one of the seventeen children of M——. And I am a delegate here, representing over one hundred Sunday-schools sprung from that one."

VI.

PERHAPS no man gets such a vivid idea of the dark and bright sides of frontier life as the general missionary. One week among the rich, entertained sumptuously, and housed with all the luxuries of hot air and water and the best of cooking; and then, in less than twelve hours, he may find himself in a lumber-wagon, called a stage-coach, bumping along over the wretched roads of a new country, and lodged at night in a log house with the wind whistling through the chinks where the mud has fallen out, to sit down with a family who do not taste fresh meat for weeks together, who are twelve miles from a doctor and as many from the post-office.

Nowhere in the world can a man so soon exchange the refinements of civilized life for one of hardship and toil

as in a new country. Our minute-man
must share with the settler all his toils,
and yet often forego the settler's hope.
The life among frontiersmen is apt to
unfit a man for other work. His scanty
salary will not allow many new books,
and often his papers are out of date.
The finding of a home is one of the worst
of hardships. Let us start with the missionary to the front; our way lies through
a rich valley. The moon is at her full,
and we pass fine farms. The scent of
the hay floats in at the car windows;
fine orchards surround the houses, while
great flocks of sheep are seen feeding,
and herds resting, comfortably chewing
the cud.

But morning comes, and we must
change cars. We are in a city of 80,000
people, with 498 factories with 15,000
employees, where a few years ago a few
log houses only were in sight. As we
change cars we change company too.
We left the train at a Union Station,
with its green lawns and trim garden, to

find a station with old oil-barrels around it, the mud all over everything, the train filled with lumbermen, with their red mackinaw shirts and great boots spiked on the bottoms, and a comforter tied around the waist.

A few women are on the train, often none at all. Our new road is poorly ballasted, and the train bounces along like a great bumble-bee. The men are all provided with pocket-pistols that are often more deadly than a revolver. At the first station — a little mouse-colored affair, sometimes without a ticket-agent — we notice the change. The stumps are thick in the fields; many of the houses have the building-paper fluttering in the wind; the streets are of sawdust. You can see the flags growing up from the swamp beneath. The saloons are numerous; and as the train is a mixed one in more senses than one, abundant time is given while shunting the freight-cars for the men to reload their pocket-pistols and get gloriously drunk.

"Kings may be blest, but Tam was glorious."

And so on we go again for forty miles, when all leave the train but one solitary man, who lies prostrate in the car, too big for our little conductor to lift, and so he goes to the terminus with us. It is getting late, and the last ten miles are through a wilderness of dead pines, with here and there a winding line of timothy and clover that has sprung up from seeds dropped by the supply teams. But presently we see a pretty stream with bosky glades, and visions of speckled trout come up; then an immense mill, and a village of white houses with green Venetian blinds, and a pert little church. We had expected some good deacon to meet us and take us home to dinner; but, alas! no deacon is waiting, or dinner either for some time. For out of eight hundred people only five church-members can be found, four of them women.

It well nigh daunts the minute-man's courage as he sees the open saloons, the big, rough men, the great bull-terriers on the steps of the houses. The awful swearing and vile language appal him, and the thought of bringing his little ones to such a place almost breaks his spirits; but here he has come to stay and work. The hotel is his home until he can find a house for his family. There is but one place to rent in the town, and that is in a fearful condition. It is afterwards whitewashed and used as a chicken-coop. But at length a family moves away, and the house is secured just in time; for the new schoolmaster is after it, and meets the man on the way with a long face.

"You got the house?"

"Yes."

"What can I do? my goods are on the way!"

"Oh, they will build one for you, but not for a preacher."

"No, they won't. Could I get my things in for eight or ten days?"

"Oh, yes." The minister is so glad to get the place that he feels generous. But

the good man stays eleven months; and he
has besides his wife and child, a mother-
in-law, a grandmother-in-law, a niece, a
protégée, and a young man, a nephew, who
has come to get an education and do the
chores. They are all very nice people, but
it leaves the minute-man and his wife and
four children with but three rooms. The
beds must stand so that the children have
to climb over the head-boards to get at
them. The family sit by the big stove at
their meals, and can look out on the glowing sand and see the swifts darting about;
while in the winter the study is sitting-
room and playground too.

But this is luxury. Often the minute-
man must be content with one room, for
which the rent charged may be extortion-
ate. Even then he must keep his water
in a barrel out in the hall. In cold weather
perhaps it must be chopped before getting it into the kettle.

I knew of one man who lived in a log
house. It had been lathed and plastered
on the inside, and weather-boarded on the

outside, so that it was very warm, and so thick that you could not hear the storms outside, which raged at times for days together.

One day late in March a fearful snow-storm arose, and for three days and nights the snow came thick and fast. Luckily it thawed fast too. On the fourth day there was need for the minute-man to go for the doctor, who lived some miles away. On the road he engaged a woman to go to his house, where her services were in demand. After he had summoned the doctor the good man took his time, and reached home in the afternoon. He was greeted by a duet from two young strangers from a far land.

Night closed in fast; the house was so thick that no one suspected another storm; but on going out to milk the cow, it was storming again, and the man saw he had need to be careful or he would not find his way back from the barn, though it was only a few yards away.

When he reached the house, the good

lady visitor, who had insisted that she could not stay later than evening, gave up all hope of getting home that night. She stayed a fortnight! For this time the storm raged without thawing, and for three nights and days the snow piled up over the windows, and almost covered the little pines, in drifts fifteen feet deep. Not a horse came by for two weeks.

Once another man started in a storm on a similar errand; but in spite of his love, courage, and despair, he was overwhelmed, and sinking in agony in the drift, he never moved again. When the storm was over, the sun came out; and what a mockery it seemed! The squirrels ran nimbly up the trees, the blue jays called merrily; but the settlers looked over the white expanse, and missed the gray smoke that usually rose from the little log shanty.

The men gathered to break the roads; the ox-team and snow-plough were brought out, and the dogs were wild with delight as they ploughed up the snow with their snouts, and barked for very joy; but the men were sorrowful, and worked as for life and death. Half way to the house the husband was found motionless as a statue, his blue eyes gazing up into the sky. The men redoubled their efforts, and gained the house. The stoutest heart quailed. A poor cat was mewing piteously in the window. And when at last the oldest man went in, he found mother and new-born child frozen to death.

VII.

THE South has two kinds of frontier,
—that which has never been settled, and
once thickly settled parts that have grown
up to wild woods and wastes since the
war. In old times the slave had a half-
holiday on Saturday, which custom the
colored brother still keeps up; and a more
picturesque scene is not to be found than
that presented by a town, say of three
thousand inhabitants, where the county
has seven colored people to one white.

Never was such a motley company gathered in one place,— old men with griz-
zled heads, all with a rabbit-foot in their
pocket, a necklace for a charm around
their necks, their bronzed breasts open
to view; old mammies with scarlet ban-
dannas; young belles of all shades — here
a mulatto girl in pale-blue dress and

pointed shoes, her waist as disfigured as any Parisian's, there a mammoth, coal-black negro driving a pair of splendid mules.

Here is an original turnout; it was once a sulky. The shafts stick out above the great ears of the mule; the seat has been replaced by an old rocking-chair; the wheels are wired-up pieces of a small barrel that have replaced some of the spokes, while fully half the harness is made up of rope, string, and wire. The owner's clothes are one mass of patch-work, and his hat is full of holes, out of which the unruly wool escapes and keeps his hat from blowing off.

The sidewalk presents a moving pano-rama unmatched for richness of color. As we leave the town, we ride past planta-tions that once had palatial residences, whose owners had from one to three thousand slaves, the little log cabins ar-ranged around and near the house. In many cases the houses are still there, but dilapidated.

Here, where each white person was once worth on an average thirty thousand dollars, to-day you may buy land for a dollar an acre, with all the buildings. It is a lovely park-like country, with clear streams running through meadows, branching into a dozen channels, where the fish dart about; and the trees shade and perfume the air with their rich blossoms, and the whole region is made exquisitely vocal with the song of the peerless mocking-bird. Here, too, the marble crops out from the soil, and some of the richest iron ore in the world, all waiting for the spirit of enterprise to turn the land into an Eldorado.

To be sure, there are obstacles; but the Southern man of to-day was born into conditions for which he is not responsible, any more than his father and ancestors before him were responsible for theirs. And those that started the trouble lived in a day when men knew no better. Did not old John Hawkins as he sailed the seas in his good ship Jesus, packed with

Guinea negroes, praise God for his great success? So we find the men of that day piously presenting their pastor and the church with a good slave, and considering it a meritorious action.

Time, with colonies settling in the new South, will yet bring back prosperity without the old taint, and keep step with all that is good in the nation. It cannot be done at once. I knew an energetic American who had built a town, and thought he would go South, and at least start another; but, said he, "I had not been there a week when I felt, as I rocked to and fro, listening to the music of the birds, and catching the fragrance of the jessamine, that I did not care whether school kept or not."

There is no great virtue in the activity that walks fast to keep from freezing. We owe a large portion of our goodness to Jack Frost.

Dr. Ryder tells a story of one of our commercial travellers who had been overtaken by night, and had slept in the home of a poor white. In the morning he naturally asked whether he could wash. "Ye can, I reckon, down to the branch." A little boy belonging to the house followed him; for such clothes and jewellery the lad had never before seen. After seeing the man wash, shave, and clean his teeth, he could hold in no longer, and said, —

"Mister, do you wash every day?"

"Yep."

"And scrape yer face with that knife?"

"Yep."

"And rub yer teeth too?"

"Yep."

"Wal, yer must be an awful lot of trouble to yerself."

Civilization undoubtedly means an awful lot of trouble.

VIII.

ALL SORTS AND CONDITIONS OF MEN.

THE frontier is the place to find all sorts of conditions and also of men. Monotony is not one of the troubles of the minute-man. He is frequently too poor to dress in a ministerial style, and quite often he is not known until he begins the services. This sometimes leads to the serio-comic, as witness the following : —

Our man was looking over a portion of the country where he wished to locate, and in making the necessary inquiries he asked many questions about homesteads and timber claims. Notice having been given that there would be preaching at the schoolhouse, the people assembled; and while waiting for the preacher, they discussed this stranger, whom they all thought to be a claim jumper. He certainly was not a very handsome man. They proposed to hang him to the first tree. Trees were scarce there, and possibly that fact saved him. He came up while they were talking, entered the schoolhouse, and from the desk told them he was the preacher, and was going to settle among them. Here was a promising field, where people were ready to hang a man on their way to church. It is a fact that where we find people ready for deeds of this kind we have the material for old-fashioned revivals of the Cartwright type.

When Jesse James was shot, it was easy to find a man to preach a sermon full of hope to the bereaved relations, and to crown the ruffian with martyrdom.

The minute-man has some hair-breadth escapes. He comes upon a crowd of so-called vigilants, who have just hanged some men for horse-thievery; and, as he has on store-clothes, he narrowly escapes the same fate. In one instance he was able to prove too late that they had hanged an innocent lad ; and in that case the poor boy had not only pleaded his innocence but had explained that he was tired, and had been invited to ride by the gang who had stolen the horses, the men themselves corroborating his story; but it did not avail; and the poor boy was strung up, and a mother's heart was broken in the far East. Often these border ruffians act from unaccountable impulse, just as the Indians would torture some captives and adopt others from mere whim.

It is an awful commentary on the condition of things on our frontiers, that a man has a better chance of escape when he has murdered a fellow creature than when he has stolen a horse. And yet in this year 1895, I have seen a man who was trying in vain to sell a horse for $1.50.

To illustrate how much more valuable life is than gold, a minister relates this anecdote of a California miner who, to save a young girl in a shipwreck, threw his belt of gold away and saved her life. After the meeting was over a matronly woman came up to him and said, "Sir, I was the young girl the miner saved." Or he enters a log house, and finds a beautiful woman and her no less beautiful daughter, and soon learns that, a few years before, they were moving among the brilliant throng that surround royalty in Europe; and in that little room the mother has the dress and some of the jewels in which she was presented to Queen Victoria. He finds them in the little log house, apparently contented; but there is a romance and a mystery here that many would like to unravel. Or, maybe, he enters the neat frame house of a broken-down Wall-street stockbroker, who with the remnants of his fortune hopes to retrieve himself upon his one hundred and sixty acre homestead, and who, with his refined and cultured family, makes an oasis in the desert for the tired missionary.

In the winter he sometimes rides a hundred miles to Conference, and time and again is upset as he attempts to pass through the immense drifts. His harness gives way when he is miles from a house; and he must patch it up as best he can from the other harness, and lead one horse. He must learn to ride a tricking broncho, to sleep out on the prairie, to cover himself with a snowdrift to keep from freezing, and in case of extremity to kill his horse and crawl inside, perhaps barely to escape with his life as the warm body changes into a refrigerator. If he lives in a sod house, he must often put the sheets above his head to keep away the lizards that crawl out as the weather becomes warm, and an occasional rattler waking up from his torpid winter sleep. At times the rains thaw his roof out, and it drops too; and then he must re-shingle with sod.

Often he is called to go forty and fifty miles to visit the sick, to sit up with the dying, and to cheer their last moments. He can and does do more useful work when attending the poor and sickly than in any other way. Many a family has been won through the devotion of the minute-man to some poor little sufferer.

One day he meets a man hauling wood with a pair of wretched mules. The man is dressed in blue denim, the trousers are stuffed into boots that are full of holes. A great sombrero hat is on his head. By his side is a beautiful young woman. She is the wife. He finds on inquiry that the man has been a brilliant preacher, writer, and lecturer; yet here, two thousand miles from his Eastern home, he is hauling railway ties for a living.

I once visited a family living in a house so small that the kitchen would barely hold more than one person at a time. There was a sick man there, whom I used to call upon two and three times a week. In order to turn himself, he had a leather strap hung from the rafters. The woman of the house was of a cruel disposition. She was the second wife of the sick man's brother, and had a daughter who was about thirteen years of age, but who was large for her years. I used to find this child working about in her bare feet and singing, "I'm so glad that my Father in heaven." And I felt quite encouraged, as the child had a bad reputation.

One day this girl came to the parsonage and brought a silver napkin-ring, saying it was a New Year's gift, and that her mother was sorry she could not have engraved upon it "For my dear *pasture.*" My wife said we ought not to take it; but I replied, —

"Yes; these people get fair wages, and would feel offended."

So we kept it. Some days after, as two men were felling a large pine-tree which was hollow at the base, they were surprised to see albums, bracelets, napkin-rings, combs, spoons, and other articles falling out. About this time a saleswoman had been missing just such things from her counter; and it was soon discovered that my youthful convert was a first-class kleptomaniac, equal to any

city thief of the same class. Her mode
of operation was to call the woman's attention to something on the shelf behind
her; then taking anything within reach,
and with an " Oh, how pretty!" she
would decamp.

I met the mother on my way to visit
the sick man. " O Elder!" she said,
"I am in a peck of trouble. That gal
of mine has cleared off on a raft with a
lumberman, and she has been stealing
too. What shall I do?"

As I knew that the woman had tied
the girl's tongue with whip-cord, and
beaten it with birch bark until it bled,
to cure her of lying, I said, " You had
better send her to the Reform School."
It appeared afterward that the man who
had run off with the girl was a minister's son; and he said in court he had
taken pity on the girl, and wanted to
save her from the cruelty of her mother.
The girl was sent to the Reform School
at Adrian, but not before she had given
the sheriff the slip, and taken another

girl with her, getting as far as Rochester, N.Y., before she was recaptured.

Sometimes in these frontier towns the sermon is stopped in a most unexpected way. I remember one good man preaching on Jacob. An old woman, who was sitting on the front bench, became deeply interested ; and when the minister said, " When the morning came, Jacob, who had served all these long years for his wife, found not the beautiful Rachel, but the weak-eyed Leah," the old lady broke out with " Oh, my God, what a pity ! " That ended the discourse, and the benediction was omitted.

In another back settlement a young student was preaching on the Prodigal Son. " And what, my friends, would you have done had your son come home in that way after such conduct ? " The answer was prompt, " I would have shot the boy, and saved the calf."

A SOUTHERN SAWMILL.

Page 91.

IX.

"You are going the wrong time of the year," was the reiterated warning of friends who heard that I was to make a Southern trip. Experience proved them to be as far astray as if they had warned one from going North in June; for the May of the South is the June of the North. Nature was revelling in her fullest dress, making a symphony in green, — all shades, from the pale tint of the chinquapin and persimmon, to the deep indigo of the long-leafed pine, and the tender purple green of the distant hills, — a perfect extravaganza of vegetable growth.

The weather was delicious; from the south and east came the ocean air, and from the north and west the balsam-laden ozone of the mountains, every turn in the road revealing new beauties. The cool Southern homes, with their wide verandas covered with honeysuckle, and great hallways running right through the house, often revealing some of the daintiest little pictures of light and shade, from apple or china tree varied with the holly, the Cape jasmine, and scuppernong vines, the latter often covering a half-acre of land, while chanticleer and his seraglio strutted in proud content, monarch of all he surveyed. High on a pole hung the hollowed gourds, homes for the martins and swallows. The mistress sat at her sewing in the shady porch, while out beyond, under a giant oak, with gracefully twined turban and brilliant dress, the sable washerwoman hung out her many-colored pieces, making altogether a scene of rural beauty seldom surpassed.

What joy to sit in the ample porch and look over the great cotton-fields with their regular rows of bluish green, variegated by the tender hue of the young corn, and a dozen shades of as many species of oak, while the brilliant tulip-tree and the distant hills, now of softest blue, contrasting with the rich, red ochre of the soil, make up a picture never to be forgotten. Cooled by the breezes that sweep through the porch, one dozes away an hour of enchantment. The negroes with their mules, in the distance, in almost every field, add to its piquancy, and often, floating on the wind, come wild snatches in weird minor notes the broken rhythm of their old Virginia reel, performed with the rollicking exuberance of the race.

The reader must not suppose that all Southern homes answer to the above description. Thousands of houses are without a porch or any shade save that which nature gives. The chimneys are built on the outside, sometimes of stone, sometimes of brick or of clay, while layers of one-inch slats hold the chimney together; but, as a rule, so prodigal is nature that a vine of some kind will

entwine around their otherwise bare and
severe outlines, and make them, like some
dogs, homely enough to be handsome.

Although these poorer houses are devoid of all artificial attempts to beautify,
they are frequently built near a great oak
and the dense china-tree for shade, while
wild fruits of many kinds grow promiscu-
ously about.   In every hedgerow, and
within a stone's throw of nearly every
country home, will be found partridges,
wild pigeons, and all sorts of small game,
with plenty of foxes to keep it in reason-
able bounds, while every household has
a number of hounds and curs for the
foxes.   But with all the varied beauty
of the scene, the New Englander constantly misses the well-kept lawn, — for
here bare ground always takes the place
of grass, — and there are no village green
and fine shaded roads, and that general
neatness which distinguishes the rural
scenes of " the Pilgrim land."

A few words about the people.   They
are as warm-hearted as their climate;

the stranger is greeted with such invita-
tions as these: "Come in;" "Take a
chair;" "Have some of the fry;" "Have
some fresh water." They are up with
the sun — family prayer by five, A.M.;
breakfast half an hour later; dinner at
one; supper at seven; to bed by dark.
The churches are plain, costing seldom
more than eight hundred or ·one thousand dollars; doors on all sides opposite
each other to allow for a good circulation
of air. A pail of water stands on a form
near the pulpit. The church generally
stands in a grove or the forest itself.

The people are very fond of preaching. The whole family, from the oldest
to the youngest, go; and one may often
see the mother at the communion with
a little one at the breast. Sometimes
eleven or more of a family will occupy
a wagon filled with oak-splint chairs.

It takes one back thirty years ago to
the West, as one stands at the church-
door and sees the people flocking in
through winding roads in the woods, the

sunlight and shadow dancing upon the moving teams that shine like satin in the bright morning air. The dogs are wild with delight as they start a covey of partridges, and make music in the deep shadows of the woods. Here a group of young men and maidens are drinking at the spring.

The preacher often is a jack-of-all-trades — sometimes a doctor, getting his degree from the family medicine-book; and strange to say, though an ardent believer in faith-cure, and with marvellous accounts of cures in answer to prayer, yet prescribing a liver invigorator when that organ is in trouble. Some of these men are natural orators, and with their bursts of eloquence often hush their hearers to holy awe and inspiration. They have one book, and believe it. No doubts trouble them. Higher criticism has never reached them. Mosaic origin of the Pentateuch is unquestioned. Moses and no other, to them, wrote the five books, including the account of his own burial.

They know nothing of pre-exilic Psalms
or Greek periods of Daniel; but all
preach Jesus, no matter whence they
draw their text. In an instant they make
a short cut for Calvary.

One brother, over eighty years of age,
walks fifteen miles, and preaches three
times. Some of his sermons take two
hours in delivery, without the aid of a
scrap of note; and the talk for days after
is on the sermon. No quarterlies, month-
lies, or weeklies lie at home to divert.
No lecturer strays to that region. Here
and there is a village house with an
organ or a piano, and, of course, a paper.

I am speaking of the rural South, — and
nearly all the South is rural, nearly all
American, even the cities, with few excep-
tions, and the operatives are Southern,
and mostly from the farms; so that one
may find a city whose operatives live in
another State, across a river, in a community numbering nearly seven thousand
souls, and most of them keeping pigs
and a cow (or, rather, not keeping them,

for they roam at their own sweet will down grassy, ungraded streets). In such a place one meets old ladies of quite respectable appearance, with the little snuffing-stick in their mouths, or a pipe; and here one small grocery shop may sell two hundred dozen of little tin snuff-boxes in a month! There are cities in the South where you will find as fine hotels and stores as any on the continent. But from any such city it is only a step to the most primitive conditions.

Let me describe a characteristic night scene near a large city. My friend met me at the depot with his little light wagon and diminutive mule, and we started for the homestead. Our road lay between banks of honeysuckle that saturated the air with its rich perfume; wild-goose plum, persimmon, bullice, and chinquapin (the latter somewhat like a chestnut, but smaller), huckleberries on bushes twelve feet high, called currants there, lined the road on either side. The house was surrounded by the *débris* of former corncribs and present ones; stables were scattered here and there in picturesque confusion. One end of the house was open, and had been waiting for years for its chimney; there was shrubbery of every kind all about. I had the usual hearty welcome and supper, and then attended the inevitable meeting in the grove.

In the glare of the setting sun everything seemed indescribably wretched; but it was May, and night came on apace. The stars in the deep blue glowed like gems; and then the queen of night on her sable throne threw her glamour over the scene, and the stencil-marked ground became a fairy scene. High perched upon a mighty oak the mistress of the grove rained music on the cool night air, — first a twitter like a chaffinch, then an aria worthy of Patti, then the deep notes of the blackbird, then a whip-poor-will, then a grand chorus of all the night-birds.

A short breathing-spell, and off on another chorus, and so the whole night through. When we awoke the music still poured from that wondrous throat of the American mocking-bird. How calm, how peaceful, was the scene, how pure the air! The lights went out from neighboring cots, and the heavenly hosts seemed to sing together once more the song of Bethlehem — but alas! Herod plots while angels sing. Not far off is another little house with its small out-buildings. This night it is occupied by a mother and three children. The father is away attending a religious meeting. The servant who usually sleeps in the house when the man is away gives a trifling excuse and sleeps in the shed. Before retiring she quietly unfastens the pin which holds the shutter. At midnight the mother is awakened from her troubled sleep and sees the shadow of a man, and then another shadow, and still another. The children shrink to the back of their bunk. Oh, what a triple crime was enacted under that peaceful sky! Morning came. The mocking-bird still sang, and cheered the returning husband.

But alas, it was a mocking song for him ; for instead of pleasant welcomes, he found his wife delirious, and his children cowering like hunted partridges in a neighbor's house. The frenzied husband, soon joined by friends made furious by the atrocious crime (so common in the South), soon hunted the ravishers of the little home; and when the moon arose the next night, the beauty of the scene was marred by three black corpses swinging from a bridge.

X.

THE NORTH-WEST.

THE first impression a man has of the North-west is like Pat's in St. Patrick's Cathedral, — " Begorra, it's bigger inside than out."

Take the map, and see what a little thin strip the upper peninsula of Michigan makes. Now start on the best train at St. Ignace in the morning, and it is eight at night before you reach the copper regions or the Gogebic Range. When I lived in St. Ignace, and the connections were poor, it took two days to travel from that port to Calumet. If we went by water we had to sail forty miles east before we doubled Point Detour; and then we threaded our way among scenes of beauty equal to the Thousand Islands of the St. Lawrence. Every mile of the way is alive with historic interest. In

St. Ignace lie the bones of Father
Marquette; across the Straits, Mackinaw City, where the terrible massacre oc-
curred, spoken of by Parkman; midway,
is Mackinaw Island, called by the Indians The Great Turtle.

Here to-day on the Island are the old
block forts, and here the little iron safe in
which John Jacob Astor kept his money
when in the fur-trade. Full of natural
beauty, to-day the past and present crowd
one another. Here are Indians, half-
breeds, and Americans, and modern hotels.
There are no mosquitoes; for the Island
is but three miles in diameter, and the
wind blows too strong for them.. Here
you may find the lilac in full bloom on
the Fourth of July, and in the fall delicious blue plums that have not been hurt
by the black knot. The daylight is
nearly eighteen hours long in midsum-
mer. The people are sowing oats when
the southern farmers in the State are
thinking of cutting theirs. In April,
near Grand Rapids, I picked the arbutus.

In early May, at Vanderbilt, I picked it again, and saw pure white snow in patches in the woods. Later in May I saw it again north of the Straits of Mackinaw, and in June I found it in the Keweenak Peninsula. At Hancock I saw a foot of snow compressed under the cordwood, and some between buildings not exposed to the sun. On account of the lateness of the season, pease escape the bugs, which are elsewhere so destructive; and thousands of bushels of seed are sent every year to the upper Peninsula.

But to return to St. Ignace. It is so unlike any other American town, that I did not wonder at an old lady of over ninety, who was born there, speaking of her visit to Detroit as the time when she went to the States. Here the old Catholic church dates back to the early days of French settlement. The lots run from the water-front back. Your Frenchman must have a water-front, no matter how narrow. So the town was four miles long, and composed mostly of one street, which followed the water-front; and although there were four thousand people living there in 1884, and we had a mayor, the primeval forest came right into the city.

The only house I could get was new, — so new that we moved in while the floors were still wet. The lumber in it was green, and we could not open the sashes for months; but before winter came, the shrinkage caused the windows to rattle like castanets. To get our furniture there, we had to cross the railway tracks twice, — once the regular road, and then the branch which ran to the great furnace at the point. And yet so new was everything in this old town, that our street had not been graded, and our wagons had to cross land where they sunk up to the axles. A few miles up the road the deer, the wolves, and black bear lived; and no less than eleven deer were seen in the road at one time near Allenville. We moved in the month of June, and put up our base-burner, and started the fire.

The climate is delicious from June to October; the air and waters are as clear as crystal. You can see fish forty feet below you, and the color of the pebbles at the bottom. There is an indescribable beauty about these northern shores; the tender green of the larch-fir, or tamarack, the different shades of blue-green among the cedars, the spruce, hemlock, and balsam, mixed with the lovely birch, and multi-colored rocks, make up some of the loveliest scenery on the continent. Little islands, so small that but one or two trees can find root, up to the islands that take hours to steam by, while the streams team with trout and grayling, the lakes with white-fish, muskalonge, and mackinaw trout and herring. Thousands of men are engaged in the fisheries, and millions of dollars are invested.

You sit at your door, and can see the home and people of old France, with their primitive canoe, and at the same time see propellers of three thousand tons' burden glide stately by.

XI.

A BRAND NEW WOODS VILLAGE.

IT does not take long to build a new village on the prairie, — the hardest work, the clearing of the ground, is already done; but here in the dense forest it is a different thing, even when the railway runs through it. First the men go in, and begin to clear the ground. It is virgin soil, and not an inch of ground but has something growing. Giant maples — some of them bird's-eye, some curly — are cut down and made into log heaps; black walnuts are burned up, that, made into veneer, would bring thousands of dollars.

Such was the state of things within twelve years. To-day it is different. The settler will take a quarter section, bark the trees to find the desired kind, cut them down, and leave for another section.

Rich companies came in, and began to devastate the forests to make charcoal, until the State had to make a law that only a certain number of acres in the hundred may be cut.

In some few cases women will go with their husbands, and sometimes one woman will find herself miles and miles away from another. I·visited one such house; and while the good woman was getting the dinner ready, I strolled about and took notes. On the rude mantel-shelf, I saw some skulls, and asked what kind of an animal they belonged to. She said,—

"Oh! them's beavers' skulls. My! I wish we had some beavers here now; I would make you some beaver-tail soup."

"Why, did you have them here since you came?"

"Oh, yes! plenty of them. When I got lonesome — and that was pretty much every day — I used to go and watch them build their dams. I don't know how they did it; but I have seen them sink a log so that it would stay put, and not come up. I tried it dozens of times, but could not do it. I had lots of time, nothing to read, and the nearest town fifteen miles away. I used to think I should go mad sometimes, and even a land-hunter coming from outside was a godsend. Indeed, I remember one coming here, and he took sick, and died in spite of all we could do. We had neither boards nor planks, nothing but logs. So we slipped two flour-barrels over him, and he looked real nice. We buried a little boy too. I keep the graves clear of weeds, and plant flowers about them, and often sit there with my work and think of those early days."

" How long ago was that ? " I asked.

" Four years ago ! Why, you know there wan't no railway then ; but now, — why, I got Zeke to cut down the trees, and I can see the trains go by with parlor cars and sleepers. There'll be one pretty soon if it is on time." And sure enough, in a few minutes a long train thundered by.

Sometimes a train stopped near us, and hundreds of men from the south of Ohio came with their dogs, guns, and men-servants, and went hunting and fishing ; and, strange as it may seem, you can find ten times as many deer to-day as you could forty years ago. The settling of new lands has driven them into closer quarters, and the game-law does much good. The State fish-hatcheries supply the streams with fry ; and at times the men sent out to stock the streams get misled by the settlers, who show them the different streams, and only too late they find they have put the whole stock of young fry into the same stream. The average conscience is not yet fine enough to see anything but a joke in this.

But to the building of our village. Often at first no house has more than one room. The men are making their homes, and will stop to cut out a piece of the log, and make a place for a little child's doll. Cupboards, too, are made in the same way.

Water is one of the indispensable necessities; and, as a rule, the town will be built on a stream, or near a spring. Sometimes wells have to be dug over a hundred feet deep. Arrow-heads, and implements of the chase, and bones of men and extinct races of animals, turn up.

In one town I visited, before the wells were dug, the water for drinking was brought in barrels on flat cars, while melted snow answered for washing.

" But what did you do when that was gone? " I asked.

" Well, the maple-sap begun to run, and then the birch, which was better; but lor! you couldn't iron nothin'."

I passed a little log house standing out of line with the street; and I thought it was a chicken-coop, and asked why it was built that way.

" My! " said the woman with a laugh, " that ain't a chicken-coop; that's our first meeting-house. Us women built that. We had one or two old men to help, and the children; and we women did the rest.

We were quite proud of it too. It cost fourteen dollars complete. For the minister's chair we cut down a barrel, and covered it with green baize."

A minister writes, "My room is one end of the garret of a log house, where I can barely stand erect under the ridgepole. My study-table and bookcase I made from rough boards. As I sit writing, I look forth from a window two by three, upon a field dotted with stumps, log huts, and charcoal kilns, and skirted with dense forests."

While I was visiting this section, a woman showed me her hands cracked with the frost. The tears came to her eyes as she said, "I tell ye it's pretty hard lines to have to milk cows when it is forty below zero." No man can imagine the arduous work and the awfulness of life in a northern winter. What is a joy to the well-dressed, well-fed man, with his warm house and the comforts of a civilized community, is often death to the poor minute-man and set-

tler on the frontier. I have sat by the
side of the minute-man, and heard from
him a story that would bring tears to
the eyes of the most cynical.

One man I shall never forget, a good
hardy Scotchman, with a brave little wife
and four children. His field was near
Lake Superior; his flock poor homesteaders and Indians. The winters have
a hundred and fifty days' sleighing; the
frost sometimes reaches 50° below zero,
and is often for days together 30° below;
so that when it suddenly rises to zero, one
can hardly believe it is freezing. Here
is his story : —

"We were twelve miles from a doctor; and towards spring two of our children complained of sore throats. It
proved to be diphtheria. We used all
the remedies we had, and also some
herbs given us by an old squaw; but
the children grew worse, and we determined to go back to the old settlement.
My wife carried the youngest, and I the
next one. The other children walked

behind, their little legs getting scratched with the briers. We had twelve miles to go to reach the steamer. When we got there, one of the little ones died; and before we reached home the other expired. We buried our two treasures among the friends in the cemetery; and after a while I said to my wife,—

"'Shall we go back to the field? Ought we to go?'

"Her answer was, 'Yes.'

"We went back. Our old parishioners were delighted to see us; and soon we were hard at work again. Winter came on, and God gave us another little one. You may be sure he had a double welcome; but as the cold became intense, our little lamb showed signs of following his brothers. I tried to keep my wife's spirits up, while I went about my work dazed. At last the little fellow's eyes seemed so large for his face, and he would look at us so pitifully, that I would break down in spite of myself.

"He died; and the ground was frozen

over six feet deep, and we had to bury him in a deep snow-bank that nearly covered our little shanty. My wife would go out nights when she could hear the wolves howling, and stand with an old Paisley shawl over her head, while I was miles away preaching to a handful of settlers in a log cabin; and when I would return I would find her there keeping watch, and sometimes I would have hard work to get her into the house. Pardon these tears, my brother, but come they will."

He need not have said it; my own were running, though my head was turned away.

Yes, we weep, and hold on to our money, while brave men and women, with their little ones, suffer for the lack of it, and lay down their lives for those who come after them. How men and women can live in fine homes, and spend ten times as much on luxuries as they give to the Lord, and still sing they love his kingdom, is more than I can understand

— except it be they don't mean what they sing.

The first thing one notices after passing the great iron clock are the odd names on some of the signs. There is the "Golden Rule" livery stable, with its attendant saloon. On its left, quaintly linking the past with the present, is an old log house, built in past century style, with its logs hewn, tongued, and grooved, but used at present as a printing-office, with the latest style of presses. One can easily imagine the time when beside its huge fireplace the half-breed and the Indian squatted, smoked their pipes, and told their stories; for it is not four years since that was so. Outside, nailed to the logs, is a coon-skin, and underneath it the legend, "Hard Cider." From this primitive place issues the democratic *Free Press*. A little farther on, and we notice "Dr. ——, horse doctor and saloon keeper." A very few more steps brings us to the Home Saloon, the Mansion House, the Clarendon, and the Young Canadian.

Besides these, there are twenty other saloons, with and without names ; you will not be surprised when I tell you that, on my first visit here, I found a poor man had cut his throat after a heavy spree. The shame he felt at the thought of meeting wife and children (who were on their way, expecting to find a home) was too much for him, and hence suicide. So when wife and little ones arrived they found only a dying husband and father.

Not long after this a young man, the only support of his parents, went out into the dark night from a dance, dazed with drink. He fell on the track, and the morning express crushed him to death. Brother Newberry, going to condole with the parents, found the poor father bedridden by an accident, and the mother, who was furious with drink, held by two men. Down on the dock, one evening, a poor man fell into the lake. He had been drinking to drown his sorrows (a man having run away with his wife). The bystanders, among whom was

his own son, seemed stupidly indifferent
to his fate; and when they did arouse
themselves it was only to bring up his
dead body. This they laid in the freight
shed, while the son went coolly to work
on a vessel close by, and brutal men
made jests of the misery of the dead
man's married life.

To give you an idea of the zest with
which the liquor traffic is carried on, let
me say that three days after the ferry-
boat "Algomah" was stuck fast in the
ice-drift, and while it was yet dangerous
to cross the strait by sleigh, a saloon
was built on the ice about a mile from
shore to catch the teamsters as they
passed with freight. When I saw it five
days later, it had been removed nearer
the shore; so that it was built and taken
down and put up again all within a
week.

But come with me out of so baneful an
atmosphere. Let us cross the Strait of
Mackinaw on the ice by moonlight. What
a scene! It is a wild midnight, the moon

at the full, a light snow falling; and although it is here only six miles to the other side, you cannot see the shore, as the snow thickens. There are miles upon miles of ice, driven by the fierce gale, sometimes into the depths, again mounting the crest of some mighty billow, groaning and cracking up into all shapes and sizes, swirling as if in some giant whirlpool, transfixed and left in all its awful confusion. It is glittering with beauty to-night; yet so wild, so weird, so awfully grand and solemn, that we involuntarily repeat, " Lord, what is man that thou art mindful of him?"

The sleighs look, in the distance, like a little dog-train. Now you are gliding over a mile of ice, smooth as glass, while all around it is heap upon heap; then you pass through gaps cut by the road-makers, who have left little pine-trees to guide you; and though the ice in places is packed thirty feet deep, you feel a sense of comfort and safety as you pass from the bleak sweep of the wind into the thick cedars on the shore, and nestle down as if in the shadow of His wing.

The next crossing is by early morn. The sun comes cheerily up from out a great cloud of orange and vermilion, while here and there are crimson clots and deep indigo-colored clouds rolling off to follow the night. I cannot describe the beauty of this scene; that needs a poet; but I can tell you of the odd side. Away we go behind two Indian ponies, snorting and prancing as if they, too, enjoyed the beauty of the scene. But look! not forty yards away is the " Algomah." After being resurrected from the ice with dynamite, she has begun her regular trips. Bravely she ploughs through two feet of blue ice; and when she comes to the high ridges backs up and charges them again and again. After hours of faithful work, she makes St. Ignace after sundown, seven miles from the spot she left at sunrise.

You will not be surprised, perhaps, to find your missionary from Northern Michigan turning up at Olivet, Southern Michigan where the Lord graciously baptized the meetings with his Holy Spirit. I collected seventy-two dollars towards a little church, to be called Olivet Chapel; and, better still, quite a number decided to be Christians. Best of all, thirteen young Christian students gave themselves to God, and will be ready when the time comes for the work of Christian missions.

At Ann Harbor I was most cordially welcomed by Brother Ryder and his church, and received from them hopeful assurance of help for our church at Sugar Island; so the time was not thrown away in going South. At Newberry, Brother Curry has been offered the use of the new church built by Mrs. Newberry of Detroit. So the Lord is opening the way. If we could only get one or two of those ministers who were seen "out West" sitting on the four posts of the newly surveyed town, waiting to build churches, we could furnish parishes already inhabited. Seney, Grand Marais, Point Detour, Drummond Island, and many more, are growing, with no churches.

The last time I visited Detour, a large mill had been finished and was running. The owners would give a lot, and help build a church. There are some good people living there. They gave me a cordial welcome and the best bed. I was very tired the first night and slept soundly; so I was surprised in the morning when the lady asked me if I was disturbed. On my saying "No," she said that on account of the rats her husband had to pull up the ladder, as they were sleeping on shakedowns; but she was glad I was not disturbed. The next night they kindly lent me a little black-and-tan terrier; so I slept, was refreshed, and started for home, promising I would send a missionary as soon as possible.

XII.

OUT-OF-THE-WAY PLACES.

IN making a visit to one Home Missionary, I found him living in a little board house, battened on the outside, but devoid of plaster. His study-table was a large dry-goods box, near the cook-stove, and on it, among other things, a type-writer. It looked somewhat incongruous; and on mentioning this, the good brother said, "Oh that is nothing; wait until it is dark and I will show you something else."

And sure enough, soon after supper he hung up a sheet, and gave me quite an elaborate entertainment with the help of a stereopticon. It seemed very strange to be seated in this little shell of a house, in such a new town among the pine stumps; and I could hardly realize my position as I sat gazing at the beautiful scenes which were flashed upon the sheet.

Across the road was a dance-house ; and we could hear the scraping of the fiddler, the loud voice calling off the dances, and the heavy thump of the dancers in their thick boots. Afterwards the missionary gave me a short account of his trials and victories on coming to the new field, and it illustrates how God opens the way when to all human wisdom it seems closed.

When he tried to hire a house, the owner wanted a month's rent in advance; but a short time after called on him and gave him the house and lot with a clear deed of the property for one dollar! At the same time he told him that there were lots of cedar posts in the woods for his garden fence, if he would cut them, and added that maybe some one would haul them for him. The missionary chopped the posts, " some one " hauled them for him, and up went the fence.

The missionary felt so rich that he asked the price of a fine cooking-stove that this man had loaned him. "Oh," he said, "I *gave* you that." The next thing was to find a place suitable to worship in — often no easy thing in a new town. At last a man said, "You can have the old boarding - house." This was said with a sly wink at the men standing by. So into the old log house went our friend, with his wife; and after a day's work with hoe, shovel, and whitewash, the place was ready. The whitewash was indispensable; for though the men had deserted it, there was still a great deal of life in it.

When the men saw the earnestness of the missionary they turned in and helped him, and became his friends; and in the old log boarding-house were heard the songs of praise instead of ribaldry, and prayers instead of curses, while Bibles and Sunday-school leaflets took the place of the *Police Gazette*.

The other field in which this brother works would delight Dr. Gladden's heart: 350 people, 17 denominations, all "mothered" by a Congregational church; and I don't know of another church under the sun that could brood such a medley under its wings. When the church was building, one might have seen a Methodist brother with a load of boards, a Presbyterian hauling the shingles, a Baptist with some foundation-stones, and a Mormon hewing the sills — not a Mormon of the "Latter-Day swindle variety," though, but a Josephite. In this place our brother had many a trial, however, before getting his conglomerate together.

The head man of the village offered to give a lot if the church would buy another; and in the meanwhile his charge was five dollars each time they used the hall. But the next time our brother went, the man gave both the lots; the next time, he said he would not charge for the hall; and finally he gave the lumber for the church. The church was finished, and a good parsonage added; and to-day fashionable summer resorters sit under its shadow, and never dream of the wild lawlessness that once reigned there.

A WINTER SCENE IN NORTHERN MICHIGAN.

Page 127.

The next new place I visited was well out into Lake Michigan, and yet sheltered by high bluffs clothed with a rich growth of forest trees, so that, notwithstanding its northern latitude, six degrees below zero was the lowest the mercury reached, up to the middle of February. This is saying much in favor of its winter climate, when we consider the fact that in the rest of the State it has often been from zero down to forty below for nearly a month at a time.

I do not remember such another month in years,—wind, snow, fires, intense cold, and disease, all combined. However, in spite of everything, the people turned out remarkably well, and I managed to preach twenty-eight times, besides giving talks to the children.

It took twelve hours of hard driving to make the forty miles between home and the appointment, and we were only just in time for the services. I was surprised to see the number present; but what looked to me like impassable drifts were nothing to people who had sat on the top of the telegraph-poles, and walked in the up-stairs windows off from a snow-bank, as they actually did four winters previously. The church here has a good building, heated with a furnace, and owns a nice parsonage where the minister lives with his wife and four children. Although it stormed every day but one, the meetings were blessed by the conversion of some, and the church rejoiced with a new spirit for work.

I next visited E——, a place seven years old, which ran up to fifteen hundred inhabitants in the first three years of its existence. It had about twelve hundred inhabitants, and ours was the only church-building in the place. When the pastor first came, there was neither church to worship in nor house to live in, save an old shingle shanty into which they went. It was so close to the railway that it required constant care in the daytime to keep the children safe, and not a little watching at night to keep the rough characters out. Quite a change for the better has taken place, and a bell now rings each night at nine o'clock to warn saloons to close.

It was a hard winter, and the storms came thicker than ever, blockading all railways, and making the walking almost impossible. Service on the first evening after the storm was out of the question, and for days after the walks were like little narrow sheep tracks. There are a great many things to contend with in these new mill towns under the best of circumstances; but when you add to the saloons and worse places, the roller skating-rink, a big fire, and diphtheria, you have some idea of the odds against which we worked.

In two places I visited, a fire broke out; and one could not but notice the ludicrous side in the otherwise terrible calamity that a fire causes in these little wooden towns in winter. The stores, built close together, look like rows of mammoth dry-goods boxes. When once fire gets a start, they crackle and curl up like pasteboard. At one fire a man carefully carried a sash nearly a block, and then pitched it upon a pile of cordwood, smashing every pane. Others were throwing black walnut chairs and tables out of the upper story; while I saw another throwing out a lamp-glass, crying out as he did so, " Here comes a lamp-glass!" as if it were a meritorious action that deserved notice.

At the other fire I saw a man wandering aimlessly about with a large paper advertisement for some kind of soap, while the real article was burning up. I could not but think how like the worldling he was — intent upon his body and minor things while his soul was in danger; and also how like is the frantic mismanagement at the breaking out of a fire to the sudden call of death to a man in his sins. To add to the misery of these houseless people during this intense cold, diphtheria was carrying off its victims, so that the schools were closed for the second time that winter. These things were used readily as excuses by those who did not wish to attend the meetings. Yet the skating-rink was in full blast. But with all these impediments, the conversions in the meetings, and the quickening of the church to more active life, more than repaid for all the trouble and disappointment.

We often hear of " the drink curse " in these places, and it is not exaggerated ; but there is one crime in these new towns of the north that to my mind is worse, and a greater barrier to the conversion of men and women. It is licentiousness. One little place not far from where I was preaching boasts of not having a single family in it that is not living openly in this sin. Although this is the worst I ever heard of, it is too true that our woods towns are thus honeycombed.

About the only hope the missionary has in many cases is in the children, even though he begins, as did one pastor that I know of, with two besides his own. He started his school in a deserted log shanty where it grew to be forty strong, and in spite of obstacles it grew. It was hard work sometimes, when the instinct of the boy would show itself in the pleasures of insect hunting with a pin along the log seats. Yet there the missionary's wife sat and taught. They soon had a nice church, paid for within the year.

I did not expect to find within six miles of a large city such a state of things as existed in Peter Cartwright's time in Michigan, but I did; and lest I should be called unfair, I will say I found there a few of the excellent of the earth.

Let me describe the meeting-place. It was in an old hall, the floor humped up in the middle; there was an old cook-stove to warm it, while a few lanterns hung among faded pine boughs gave out a dim light. A few seats without backs completed the furniture. Here it was that a good brother, while preaching, had the front and rear wheels of his buggy changed, making rough riding over roads none too smooth at their best. Another from the Y. M. C. A. rooms of the neighboring city had his buffalo robes stolen and every buckle of the harness undone while he was conducting services.

Knowing these things, I was not surprised at finding a rough old Roman Catholic Irishman trying to make a disturbance; but a kind word or two won him over to good behavior. Much less tractable were the young roughs, who reap all the vices of the city near by, and get none of its virtues. I had to tell them of the rough places I had seen, and that this was the first place I had been where the young men did not know enough to behave themselves in church. Promising without fail to arrest the first one that made a disturbance, I secured quiet. Of course I had to make friends with them afterwards and shake hands. Oh, how hard it is to preach the gospel after talking law in that fashion; but, friends, think how much it is needed. As a little bit of bright for so black a setting, let me say, that on the second night some kind friends substituted a box-stove for the cook-stove, lamps for lanterns, and an organ to help in the praise.

XIII.

COCKLE, CHESS, AND WHEAT.

RATHER a strange heading! I know it; but I have lost an hour trying to think of a better; and is not society composed (figuratively speaking) of cockle, chess, and wheat? In old settled parts and in cities we see society like wheat in the bulk. The plump grain is on top, but there are cockle and chess at the bottom. On the frontier the wheat is spread on the barn floor, and the chess and cockle are more plainly seen. As the fanning-mill lets the wheat drop near it and the lighter grains fly off, so in the great fanning-mill of the world, the good are in clusters in the towns and settled country, while the cockle and chess are scattered all over the borders. Of course in screenings, there is always considerable real wheat, though the grains are

small.   Under proper cultivation, however, these will produce good wheat.
These little grains among the screenings
are the children, and they are the missionaries' hope.

In my pastoral work I have met with
all kinds of humanity,—here a man living
a hermit life, in a little shanty without
floor or windows, his face as yellow as
gold, from opium; there an old man
doing chores in a camp, who had been
a preacher for twenty-five years; here a
graduate from an Eastern college, cashier
of a bank a little while ago, now scal-
ing lumber when not drunk; occasionally
one of God's little ones, striving to let
his light shine o'er the bad deeds of a
naughty world.

It was my custom for nearly a year to
preach on a week-night in a little village
near my home, sometimes to a houseful,
oftener to a handful.   Few or many, I
noticed one man always there; no matter
how stormy or how dark the night, I
would find him among the first arrivals.

He lived farther from the meeting than I, and it was not a pleasant walk at any time. One was always liable to meet a gang of drunken river-men spoiling for a fight; and there was a trestle bridge eighty rods in length to walk over, and the ties in winter were often covered with snow and ice.

Then after reaching the schoolhouse the prospect was not enchanting; windows broken, snow on the seats, the room lighted sometimes with nothing but lanterns, one being hung under the stove-pipe. Under these circumstances I became very much interested in the young man. He never spoke unless he was spoken to, and then his answers were short, and not over bright; but as he became a regular attendant on all the means of grace, — Sunday-school, prayer-meetings, and the preaching of the Word, — I strove to bring him to a knowledge of the truth, and was much pleased one evening to see him rise for prayers. As he showed by his life and conversation that he had met with a change (he had been a drunkard), he was admitted into the church, and some time after was appointed sexton.

One night, on my way to prayer-meeting, I saw a dark object near the church which looked suspicious. On investigation it proved to be our sexton, with his face terribly disfigured, and nearly blind. Some drunken ruffian had caught him coming out of the church, and, mistaking him for another man, had beaten him and left him half dead. I took the poor fellow to the saloons, to show them their work. They did not thank me for this; but we found the man, and he was " sent up" for ninety days.

Soon after this in my visits I found a new family, and I wish I could describe them. The old grandmother, weighing about two hundred pounds, was a sight, — short, stocky, with piercing eyes, and hair as white as wool. She welcomed me in when she heard that I was "the minister," and brought out her hymn-book, and had me sing and pray with her. She belonged to one of the numerous sects in Pennsylvania. She said it was a real treat to her, as she was too fleshy to get to church, and with her advancing years found it hard to walk. I found out afterward, however, that this did not apply to side-shows. From her I learned the young man's history. He had lost his parents when young; but not before they had beaten his senses out, and left him nearly deaf; and he was looked upon as one not "right sharp." Afterwards he was concerned in the murder of an old man, and was sent to State prison for life. He was brother to the old woman's daughter-in-law, an innocent looking body. There were several children, bright as dollars.

The old lady informed me that she had another son in town whom I must visit. I did so; and found him living with his family in a little house (?), the front of which touched the edge of the bank, the back perched on two posts, with a deep ravine behind, where the water ebbed and flowed as the dams were raised and lowered. I made some remarks on the unhealthiness of the location; and the man said, "It's curious, but you can smell it stronger farther off than you can close by!" I thought, what an illustration of the insidious approaches of sin! He was right, so far as the senses were concerned; but his nose had become used to it. I was not surprised to be called soon after to preach a funeral sermon there. One of the daughters, a bright girl of twelve years, had died of malignant diphtheria. It was a piteous sight. We dared not use the church, and the house was too small to turn round in, what with bedsteads, cook-stove, kitchen-table, and coffin. On the hillside, with logs for seats, we held the service.

It was touching to see the mute grief of some of the little ones; one elder sister could with difficulty be restrained from kissing the dead. She was a fine girl in spite of her surroundings, and in her grief, in a moment of confidence, said her uncle had murdered a man down South, and it preyed on her mind; but she was afraid to tell the authorities, for the uncle had threatened to kill her if she told. This confession was made to the woman she was working for; and though I did not think it unlikely, I treated it as gossip. But with the facts related in the former part of this chapter before me, I have no doubt that she spoke the truth. One murderer has gone to meet the Judge of all the earth; the other is in State prison for life.

The cockle and chess are gone; but the wheat (the children) are left, — bright, young, pliant, strong, — what shall we do with them? Let them grow more cockle instead of wheat, and chess instead of barley? Or shall they be of the wheat to be gathered into the Master's garner? If you desire the latter, pray ye the Lord of the harvest that he will send more laborers into the harvest.

I once saw an old farmer in Canada who offered ten dollars for every thistle that could be found on his hundred acres. I have seen him climb a fence to uproot thistles in his neighbor's field. When asked why he did that extra work, he said, because the seeds would fly over to *his* farm. Was he not a wise man?

Perhaps no greater danger threatens our Republic to-day than the neglect of the children — millions of school age that are not in school, and in the great cities thousands who cannot find room. Is it any wonder that we have thirty millions of our people not in touch with the church?

XIV.

CHIPS FROM OTHER LOGS.

In the Rev. Harvey Hyde's " Reminiscences of Early Days," occurs the following interesting notes : —

" In the spring of 1842 I made a horseback journey across the State (Michigan), from Allegan to Saginaw, up the Grand River Valley, past where now Lansing boasts its glories, but where then in the dense forests not a human dwelling was to be seen for many miles, on to Fentonville. Coming on Saturday night to a lonely Massachusetts tavern-keeper, I found a hearty welcome to baked beans and brown bread, and preached on the Sabbath in his barroom to his assembled neighbors — the first minister ever heard in the neighborhood. Arriving at Saginaw, after a ride for miles through swamps, with from six to ten inches of

water, sometimes covered with ice, at
the close of a March day I found myself
on the east side of the broad river,
with not a human being or dwelling in
sight, darkness already fallen, and only
twinkling lights on the other side. It
seemed a cold welcome ; but after much
shouting and waiting, kind friends appeared. Man and horse were cared for,
and two pleasant years were spent there.

" My nearest ministerial neighbor of any
denomination was twenty-five miles off on
one side, and as far as the North Pole on
the other. To a funeral or a wedding a
fifteen-mile ride was a frequent occurrence.
Many scenes come back to memory, some
provocative of sadness, some of mirth.
We were raising the frame of our new
church-building one Monday afternoon,
when a stranger came with a call to ride
twenty-five miles alone through an unknown wood-road without a clearing for
sixteen miles, to cross the Kalamazoo
River by ferry at midnight, with the ferry-
man asleep on the other bank, and the

mosquitoes abundant and hungry — to preach, and commit to the grave the bodies of eight men, women, and children who had been drowned on the Sabbath by the upsetting of a pleasure-boat. Such a sight have my eyes never looked upon, where all felt that God had rebuked their Sabbath-breaking. This was near Lake Michigan.

"Passing across the State, exchanging one Sabbath with Rev. O. S. Thompson of St. Clair, after retiring to rest for the night, I was aroused by a cry from Mrs. Thompson; and descending with speed, found that, hearing steps on her piazza, she had discovered the door ajar, and a huge bear confronting her on the outside. She slammed the door in his face, and cried for help. I looked outside, examined the pig-pen, to find all safe; no bear was visible. Returning to bed again, I was dropping to sleep, when a more startling shriek called me to look out of the window; and I saw the bear just leaping the fence, and making for the woods. This time he had placed his paws on the window at Mrs. Thompson's bedside, and was looking her in the face; and the prints of his muddy feet remained there many days. On the following Monday we were greeted by a bride and groom, who, with their friends, had crossed the river from Canada to get married. One being a Catholic, and the other a Protestant, the priest would not marry them without a fee of five dollars, which they thought too much. I married them, and received the munificent sum of seventy-five cents.

"I have had too sorrowful proof that prayers, even from the pulpit, are not always answered. On one occasion our house of worship was borrowed for a funeral by another denomination. Going late, I slipped in behind the leader at prayer as quietly as possible, to hear the petition that 'God would make the minister of this church a perfect gentleman, and surround his church with a halo of *cheveau-de-frise.*' The first I am sure was not answered; I am not sure about the others.

"Of personal hair-breadth escapes from sudden death my wife kept a record until she got to fifteenthly, and then stopped. Twice from drowning, twice from being run over by a loaded wagon, the last time the hind wheel stopping exactly at my head, but utterly spoiling my best silk hat, and showing the blessing of a good stout head."

The place where this man reined up his horse in the swamp, and had to call for a ferry, and where neither dwelling nor human being was in sight, is to-day for twenty miles almost a continuous city along the river bank. Everything is changed except the black flies and mosquitoes, which are as numerous as ever. Now, one other thing, and a curious fact too. You might dig all day and not find a worm to bait your hook, where to-day a spadeful of earth has worms enough to last the day; and this is true of all new countries. I have sent thirty-five miles for a pint of worms — all the way from St. Ignace to Petoskey; and however much the worms may have had to do with the vegetable mould of the earth, it is only where human beings live that the common angle-worm is found.

The incident of the wedding calls to mind one I heard of by a justice of the peace, a rough drinking-man, who before the advent of our minute-man performed all the marriage ceremonies. A young couple found him at the saloon. His first question was, " Want to be married ? " — " Yes." — " Married, two dollars, please, — nuff said."

A few miles above this place the first minister who went in was so frightened the next morning that he took to his heels, leaving his valise behind. The landlady, a Roman Catholic, put the boys up to pretend they were going to shoot him, and so fired their revolvers over his head ; he felt it was no place for him, and away he went. Indeed, it was as well for him that he did go ; for often, after

they were drunk, what was commenced in
fun ended in real earnest. However, I
will say this for the frontiersman, rough
as he often is, he respects a true man,
but is quick to show profound contempt
for any man of the "Miss Nancy" order.

Ireland is not the only country that
suffers from absentee landlords. The difference in the lumber-camps is often determined by the foreman. I have known
places where the owners of a large tract
of land were clergymen, and the foreman
was an infidel. His camp was a fearful
place on Christmas Eve. Twelve gallons
of whiskey worked the men up until they
acted like demons. In the morning men
were found with fingers and thumbs bitten
off, eyes gouged out, and in some few cases
maimed for life. In other places I have
known a good foreman or boss to hitch up
the teams and bring enough men down on
Sunday evening to half fill the little mission church.

There ought to be in all the lumber-
camps a first-class library, and suitable

amusements for the men; for when a few days of wet weather come together, there is nothing to hold them, and away they go in companies of six, seven, and a dozen, and meet with others from all directions, making for the village and the saloons; and then rioting and drunkenness make a pandemonium of a place not altogether heavenly to start with. I have known men who were religious who had to retire to the forest to pray, or be subjected to the outrageous conduct of their fellow workmen.

One man whom I knew kicked his wife out-of-doors because she objected to having dances in their home. She was his second wife, and was about to become a mother, but died, leaving her little one to the tender mercies of a brutal father. I remember preaching a rather harsh sermon at the funeral; but some years after I found the sermon had a mission. I met the man some hundreds of miles north. When he saw me he said he had never forgotten the sermon, and added, to my surprise, that he was a Christian now, and living with his first wife!

How men can lead such lives, involving the misery of others, and often compassing their death, and afterwards live happily, I cannot understand, except for the fact that often for generations these people have been out of the reach of Christian civilization, and so far as morals are concerned have been practically heathen. Yet, after all, I am not sure but that, in the day of judgment, they will be judged less harshly than those who have neglected to send the gospel to them.

XV.

I HAD been exploring nearly every part of the Upper Peninsula where there was any chance of an opening for Christian work ; had visited thirteen churches, and held meetings with most of them ; had a few conversions and two baptisms. I found the villages and towns on the Chicago and North-Western Railway nearly all supplied. There was one place with 1,500 people, and another with 2,000. The former had a Baptist church with about twenty members, and a Methodist Episcopal with about fifteen. The Baptists were building. The rest were more or less Lutheran, Catholic, and Nothingarian.

Surely there is need of mission work here, *but* — There are large new-fashioned mills here, with forty years' cutting ahead of them at the rate of fifty million feet of lumber per year. I had excellent audiences here and at Thompson, six miles away, where there was no church. Between these two places is Perryville, with 200 people and no church. Both are lumbering-towns.

Another town of importance is Iron Mountain, which then had 2,000 people; two Methodist churches, one Swedish, the other English-speaking. The place was alive with men and full of sin. Where are the right men to send to such places? If one sits in his study and consults statistics, they are plenty; but when you come down to actual facts, they are not to be found. "The Christian League of Connecticut" has much truth in it, but not all the truth. Without doubt their unwise distribution has much to do with "the lack of ministers;" but it is still a lamentable fact that the laborers *are* few. Not with us alone. The oft-repeated saying that "the Methodist church has a place for every man, and a man for every church," is to be taken with a grain of salt. I meet men every week who tell me they have five, seven, nine, and even eleven charges. We have a thousand just such places.

Now, if churches will put up with the fifth, seventh, ninth, or eleventh part of a man, they can have " a church for every minister, and a minister for every church." This unchristian way of pushing and scrambling in our little villages goes a long way to explain the dearth of men on the frontier ; and the seizing on " strategic points" in a new country often presents a sad spectacle.

I was much perplexed about one place. Our minister was the first on the ground ; the people voted for a union church and for him ; yet two other churches organized. When I visited the place I found our brother with a parsonage half built. There was nothing but the bare studding inside — no plaster, winter coming on, and his little ones coughing with colds caught by the exposure. Then, to crown all, the house was found to be on the wrong lot, which brought the building to a stand-still; after that two other denominations rushed up a building — one only a shell, but dedicated. There was only a handful of hearers, and our minister preached more than two-thirds of the sermons there. We had the best people with us; and yet it was plain to me there was one church more than there ought to be. Had we not been first there, and things as they were, I should say, "Arise, let us go hence!"

I am constantly asked, "When are you going to send us a man?" and we have places where there is only one minister for two villages. Ah, if the pastors hanging around our city centres only knew how the people flock to hear the Word in these new places, surely they would say, "Here am I, Lord; send me."

In one place I went to, there were two women who walked eight miles to hear the sermon. One of them was the only praying person for miles around, and for some years back the only one to conduct a funeral service, to pray, or to preach. At this place there was an old lady who came nine miles every Sunday on foot, and sometimes carried her grandchild. Think of that, you city girls in French-heeled boots! In another place of two hundred people, where there was no church, a little babe died. The mother was a Swede, only a little while out. Would you believe it, there was not a man at the funeral! Women nailed the little coffin-lid down, and women prayed, read the Scriptures, and lowered the little babe into a grave half filled with water.

In another new settlement I visited, they were so far from railway or stage that they buried a man in a coffin made of two flour-barrels, and performed the funeral rites as best they could. But these people have great hearts — bigger than their houses. When a brother minister was trying to find a place for me to stay, a man said, " Let him come with me." — " Have you room ? " — " Lots of it." So I went. In a little clearing I found the most primitive log house I ever saw ;

but the "lots of room"—that was out-of-doors. The man and his wife told me that when they came there it was raining; so they stripped some bark from a tree, and, leaning it against a fallen log, they crept underneath; and for three days it rained. The fourth being Sunday and a fine day, the settlers mocked them for not building. On Monday and Tuesday it rained again; "but we were real comfortable; weren't we, Mary?" said the man.

Then he and Mary built the house together. There was only one room and one bed; but they took off the top of the bedding, and put one tick on the floor. "That's for me," I thought. Not a bit of it. I was to have the place of honor. So, hanging some sheets on strings stretched across the room, they soon partitioned off the bed for me. Then, after reading and prayers, the man said, "Now, any time you are ready for bed, Elder, you can take that bed." But how to get there? First I went out and gave them a chance; but they did not take it. I thought perhaps they would go and give me a chance; but they did not. So I began to disrobe. I took a long while taking off coat and vest; then slowly came the collar and neck-tie; next came off my boots and stockings. Now, I thought, they will surely step out; but no; they talked. and laughed away like two children. Slipping behind the sheet, and fancying I was in another room, I balanced myself as well as I could on the feather bed, and managed to get off the rest of my clothes, got into bed, and lay looking at the moonbeams as they glanced through the chinks of the logs,. and thinking of New England with her silk bed-quilts and bath-rooms, till, as I mused, sleep weighed down my drowsy eyelids, and New England mansions and Michigan log huts melted into one, and they both became one Bethel with the angels of God ascending and descending.

I visited Lake Linden, and found the people ready for organization as soon as they could have a pastor. A brother had just left for this field; and I thought it safe to say that we should have a self-supporting church there at no distant day. We did. While staying there a man came after me to baptize two children. I went, and one would think he had been suddenly transferred to Germany. Great preparations had been made. I noticed a large bowl of lemons cut up, and the old ladies in their best attire. I was requested to give them a baptismal certificate, and to sign the witnesses' names, as they said that was done by the minister. It was a delicate way of telling me they could not write.

But that was not the strangest part of the ceremony. The father and mother stood behind the witnesses, the latter being two men and two women. The women held the children until all was ready, then handed them to the men, who held them during baptism. I preached to them a short sermon of five minutes or so, and then, when I had written the certificate, each witness deposited a dollar on the table. The father was about to hand me five dollars; but I made him give four of it to the children. They would not take a cent of the witness money; that would be "bad luck," they said. It was a new experience to me. The people had no Bible in the house. As I had left mine at the village, I had to use what I had in my heart. Here again, I thought, what work for a colporteur?

A great work might be done by one or two men who could travel all the time with Bibles and other good books, and preach where the opportunity offered. We might not see the result, but it would be just as certain; and though the people might not stay here, they will be somewhere. There are many places where neither railway, steamboat, nor stage ever reaches, and yet the people have made and are making homes there. They went up the rivers on rafts, and worked their way through the wilderness piecemeal. Missionary Thurston carried his parlor stove slung on a pole between himself and another man.

At one place, while preaching, I noticed a man fairly glaring at me. At first I thought he was an intensely earnest Christian, but he " had a devil." After meeting he told the people, " If that man talks like that to-night, I'll answer him right out in meeting." He came, and behaved himself. Some time after he had to leave town on account of a stabbing-affray, and I lost sight of him for a while. Long after I was in another place, one hundred and twenty miles away; and while talking with our missionary there, I saw a man coming from a choir-practice. I said, " Is that their minister?"

" No ; he is our new school-teacher."

" Why," I said, " that is the very man I was talking to you about, who was so wroth with the sermon."

" Oh, no! you are mistaken; he is a very pious young man — opens school with prayer, and attends all our meetings; and I know it is not put on to please the trustees, for they are not that kind of men." But it *was* the same man, minus the devil, " for behold he prayeth."

At another place I preached in a little log schoolhouse. Close to my side sat a man who would have made a character for Dickens. He had large, black, earnest eyes, face very pale, was deformed, and, with a little tin ear-trumpet at his ear, he listened intently. I was invited by his mother to dine with them. I found, living in a little house roofed with bark, the mother and two sons. One of the boys was superintendent of the Sunday-school. I was surprised at the first question put by my man with the ear-trumpet, —

" Elder, what do you think of that sermon of ——'s in Chicago? I have always been bothered with doubts, and that unsettled me worse than ever."

Who would have thought to hear, away up in the woods, in such a house, from such a man, such a question? I tried to take him away from —— to Christ. After dinner he opened a door and said, " Look here."

There, in a little workshop, was a diminutive steam-engine, of nearly one-horse power, made entirely by himself; the spindles, shafts, steam-box, and everything finished beautifully. The shafts and rods were made with much pains from large three-cornered files. He was turning cant-hook and peevy handles for a living, and to pay off the debt on their little farm. The brother had a desk and cabinet of his own make, which opened and shut automatically. I was delighted. They were hungry for books and preaching. Are not such people worth saving?

These conditions existed over twelve years ago, but they are as true to-day in all parts of the newer frontiers. Meanwhile some of the above churches have become self-supporting, and are supporting a minister in foreign lands.

XVI.

In a former chapter I was just starting for the copper regions. Come with me, we will board the train bound for Marquette.

For some miles our way ran through thick cedar forests; then we reached a hard-wood region where we found a small village and a number of charcoal kilns; a few miles farther on, another of like character. Then, with the exception of a way station or siding, we saw no more habitations of men until we reached the Vulcan iron furnace of Newberry, fifty-five miles from Point St. Ignace. The place had about 800 population, mostly employed by the company.

Twenty-five miles farther on we reached Seney, where we stayed for dinner. This is the headquarters for sixteen lumber camps, with hundreds of men working in the woods or on the rivers, year in and year out. They never hear the gospel except as some pioneer home missionary pays an occasional visit. There are some 40,000 men so employed in Northern Michigan.

After another seventy-five miles we glided into picturesque Marquette, overlooking its lovely Bay, a thriving city of some 7,000 population, the centre of the iron mining region. Here we had to wait until the next noon before we could go on.

Our road now led through the very heart of the iron country. Everything glittered with iron dust, and thousands of cars on many tracks showed the proportions this business had attained. We have been mounting ever since leaving Marquette, and can by looking out of the rear window see that great "unsalted sea," Lake Superior.

We soon reached Ishpeming, with its 8,000 inhabitants. A little farther on we passed Negaunee, claiming over 5,000 people, where Methodism thrives by reason of the Cornish miners. After passing Michigamme we saw but few houses.

Above Marquette the scenery changes; there are rocks, whole mountains of rocks as large as a town, with a few dead pines on their scraggy sides; we pass bright brown brooks in which sport the grayling and the speckled trout. Sometimes a herd of deer stand gazing with astonishment at the rushing monster coming towards them; then with a stamp and a snort they plunge headlong into the deep forest. Away we go past L'Anse, along Kewenaw Bay, and at last glide between two mighty hills the sides of which glow and sparkle with great furnace fires and innumerable lamps shining from cottage windows, while between lies Portage Lake, like a thread of gold in the rays of the setting sun; or, as it palpitates with the motion of some giant steamboat, its coppery waters gleam with all the colors of the rainbow.

Just across this narrow lake a royal welcome awaited us from the pastor of the First Congregational Church of Hancock. This fine church is set upon a hill that cannot be hid. The audience fills the room, and pays the closest attention to the speaker. They had the best Sunday-school I ever saw. Everything moved like clockwork; every one worked with vim. In addition to the papers that each child received, seventy-five copies of the *Sunday School Times* were distributed to the teachers and adult scholars. The collection each Sunday averaged over three cents a member for the whole school, to say nothing of Christmas gifts to needy congregations, and memorial windows telling of the good works in far-off fields among the mission churches. It was my privilege to conduct a few gospel meetings which were blessed to the conversion of some score or more of souls who were added to the church.

Thirteen miles farther north, and we were in the very heart of the Lake Superior region. It had been up-hill all the way. We went on the Mineral Range narrow gauge railway; but at broad-gauge price, five cents a mile, and no half-fare permits; so we were thankful to learn the little thing was only thirteen miles long.

Here we are in Calumet. At the first glance you think you are in a large city; tall chimney stacks loom up, railways crossing and recrossing, elevated railways for carrying ore to the rock-houses, where they crush rock enough to load ten trains of nearly forty cars per day, for the stamping-works of the Calumet and Hecla Company. You cannot help noticing the massive buildings on every hand, in one of which stands the finest engine in the country — 4,700 horse-power — that is to do the whole work of the mines. Everything about these great shops works easily and smoothly.

At the mine's mouth we look down and see the flashing of the lights in the miners' hats as they come up, twelve feet at a stride, from 3,000 feet below; hear the singing as it rolls up from the hardy Cornish men like a song of jubilee. Come to the public school and listen to the patter of the little feet as nearly 1,600 children pour out of their great schoolhouse, and you will be glad to know there are good churches here for training the little ones. Calumet, Red Jacket, and its suburbs cannot have much less than 10 000 inhabitants.

But here comes the minister of the Congregational church, with a hearty Scotch welcome on his lips as he hurries us into the snug parsonage, and makes us forget we ever slept in a basswood house partitioned with sheets. Here, too, we stayed and held a series of meetings. This is one of the few frontier churches that sprung, Minerva-like, full armed for the work. Never receiving, but giving much aid to others, it has increased. Here, too, I found another best Sunday-school. In this school on Sunday are scattered good papers as thick as the snowflakes on the hills ; and the 300 scholars have packed away in their hearts over 52,000 verses of the Bible, that will bring forth fruit in old age. It is rich, too, in good works — one little girl gave all her Christmas money to help build the parsonage. Over a hundred of the young people came out in the meetings, and signed a simple confession of faith; fifty of them went to the Methodist church, the rest remained with us.

From this place we go to Lake Linden, on Torch Lake, where are the stamping-works of the Calumet and Hecla mines. This company have some 2,000 men in their employ, and expend some $500,000 per year on new machinery and improvements. Everything in this place is cyclopean; ten great ball stamps, each weighing 640 lbs., with other smaller ones, shake the earth for blocks away as their ponderous weight crushes the rocks as fast as men can shovel them in. Each man works half an hour, and is then relieved for half an hour. Over 300 carloads of ore are required daily to keep these monsters at work, day and night the year round, except Sundays. A stoppage here of an hour means $1,000 lost. One stands amazed to see the foundations of some new buildings — bricks enough for a block of houses, 2,000 barrels of Portland cement and trap-rock are mixed, the whole capped off with Cape Ann granite. Two wheels, 40 feet in diameter, are to swing round here, taking up thousands of gallons of water every minute.

XVII.

SAD EXPERIENCES.

FOURTEEN years ago I attended fifty-one funerals in twenty-one months. This large number was due to the fact that toward the south and west the nearest minister was ten miles off, north and east over twenty miles; and though there were only some 450 souls in White Cloud, we may safely put down 3,000 as the number who looked to this point for ministerial aid in time of trouble.

The traveller by rail passes a few small places, and may think that between stations there is nothing but a wilderness, for such it often appears. He would be surprised to learn that one mile from the line, at short intervals, are large steam-mills with little communities — forty, fifty, and sixty souls.

Here and there are many of the Lord's people, who, overwhelmed by the iniquity they see and hear, have hung their harps upon the willows, and have ceased to sing the Lord's song. They feel that if some one could lead, they would follow; and the call for help is imperative, if we take no higher grounds than that of self-protection. Hundreds of children are growing up in ignorance, and will inevitably drift to the cities. It is from these sources that the dangerous classes in them are constantly augmented.

It is hard to believe that in our day, in Michigan, should be found such a spiritual lack as the following incident reveals. One night just as I was falling asleep, a knock aroused me. A man had come for me to go some five miles through the woods to see a poor woman who was dying. The moon was shining when we started, and we expected soon to reach the place. But we had scarcely reached the forest when a storm broke upon us. The lightning was so vivid that the horse came to a stand. The trees moaned and bent under the heavy wind, and threatened to fall on us. No less than seven trees fell in that road some few hours later. Our lantern was with difficulty kept alight, so that we made but little progress; for it was dangerous to drive fast, and, indeed, to go slow, for that matter. We spent two hours in going five miles. As we were fastening the horse, I heard cries and groans proceeding from the house, and was met at the door with exclamations of sorrow, and, "Oh, sir, you are too late, too late!"

This was an old, settled community of farmers; some eight or ten men and women at the house, some of whom have had Christian parents, and yet not one to pray with the poor woman or point her to the Lamb of God.

Did they think I could absolve her? Did they look upon a minister as a telegraph or a telephone operator, whom they must call to send the message?

We often read of the overworked city

pastor, and the contrast of his busy life with the quiet of his country brother. But the contrast does not apply to the home missionary who has a large field, as most of them have. Let me give some incidents of one week of home missionary experience. On Saturday, a funeral service. Sabbath, two Sunday-schools and preaching. Monday, I visited a poor Finnish woman, suddenly bereft of her husband, who had been fishing on Sunday in company with three others — a keg of beer which they took with them explained the trouble. Tuesday, attended the funeral, closing the service just in time to catch the train to reach an appointment nine miles off. Friday, received a telegram to come immediately to a village, where a man was killed in the mill. While there, waiting for the relatives, expected on the next train, another telegram came from home, calling me back instantly.

Yet we cannot stop, for the work presses. Did we not know that the Lord is above the water floods, we should be overwhelmed.

I am tempted to write a few lines about a family that came to Woodville just before Christmas. It consisted of a mother, son-in-law, three daughters, and two sons. Before they had secured a house their furniture (save a stove and a few chairs) was burned. They were very poor, and moved the few things they had left into two woodsheds, one of which was lower than the other, so that after the end of one was knocked out there was a long step running right across the house. Now, fancy a family of six in here in winter time, with no bedsteads, a table, and some broken chairs and stove, and you can imagine what sort of a home it was. The widow felt very despondent, hinted about being tired of life, and mentioned poison. One morning, after drinking a great quantity of cold water, she turned in her bed and died. The coroner's jury pronounced it dropsy of the heart, and waived a *post-mortem* examination.

I felt much drawn toward the children during the funeral service, and spoke mainly to them. They seemed to drink in every word, and I believe understood all.

Three weeks later a daughter lay dying of diphtheria. She called the doctor, and told him she was going home to live with Jesus, and was quite happy. One week from that time a son followed, twelve years of age. He also went quite resigned. I shall never forget the scene presented at this time; the dark room, the extemporized bedsteads, the wind playing a dirge through the numerous openings, the man worn out with night-work and watching, stretched beside the coffin, the dead boy on the other bed, two more children sick with the same disease. People seemed afraid to visit them. I gave the little ones some money each time I went. The little four-year-old, a pretty boy, said, —

" You won't have to give any for Willie this time, I have his."

Death seemed to have no terrors for the little ones. I talked to them of Jesus, and told them he was our Elder Brother and God was our Father. The little boy listened as I talked of heaven, and seemed very thoughtful. In another week, to a day, I was there again. The little fellow was going too; and now he said, —

" I want you to buy me a pretty coffin, won't you? and put nice leaves and flowers in it. I am going to heaven, you know, and I shall see my brother. Jesus is my brother, you know."

And so he passed away like one falling to sleep. I could not but think of the glorious change for these little ones, now "safe in the arms of Jesus." From a hut to a mansion, from hearing the hoarse, gruff breathing of the mill to the chanting of the heavenly choirs, from the dark squalor and rags to see the King in his beauty, to hunger no more, to thirst no more, neither to have the sun light on them nor any heat, to be led to living fountains of waters, to have all tears wiped from their eyes — who would wish them back?

I remember in one case a man whose wife had run off with another man, and had left him with two boys, one an idiot. The poor little child was found dead under the feet of the oxen, and when the funeral took place the man with his remaining son came through the woods and across lots to the cemetery, while a man with the coffin in a cart came by the road. The only ones at the funeral were these two and the carter, with myself.

I visited one home where nine out of eleven were down with diphtheria. Two young girls in a fearful condition were in the upper rooms; nothing but horse-blankets were hung up in the unplastered rooms, but they did not keep out the snow. The father and the man who drove were the only ones beside myself at this funeral. In one family four died before the first was buried.

It made me think of the plague in Lon-

don, and the man tolling the bell and crying, " Bring out your dead." Scarlet fever,
small-pox, and typhoid were epidemic for
some time, and it was then the people
began to appreciate the services of the
minute-man.

Some cases were rather odd, to say the
least. One night a boy was lost. I sug-
gested to his mother that he might be
drowned, and that the pond ought to
be searched. Her reply was amazing:
" Well, if he's drownded, he's drownded,
and what's the use till morning." Here
was philosophy. Yet at the funeral this
woman was so punctilious about the
ceremonies that, seeing a horse which
broke into a trot for a few steps, she
said " it didn't look very well at a funeral
to be a-trottin' hosses."

XVIII.

A SUNDAY ON SUGAR ISLAND.

SUGAR ISLAND is about twelve miles from Sault Ste. Marie. It is twenty-four miles long and from three to twelve wide. Its shape is somewhat like an irregularly formed pear. Seven-tenths of its people are Roman Catholic; quite a number of them came from Hudson's Bay, and what others call a terrible winter is to them quite mild.

One Scotchman, who lived there thirty years, had never seen a locomotive or been on board of a steamboat, although numbers of the latter might be seen daily passing his house all summer long, — little tugs drawing logs, and the great steamers of the Canadian Pacific Railway, with their powerful engines, and lighted by electricity. He came by way of Hudson's Bay, which accounts for his never having seen a locomotive; and he rather prided himself on never having been on board a steamboat. Like many of the trappers of an early day, he married an Indian woman. Quite a number of the descendants of these old pioneers live on the island. Some of them formed part of Brother Scurr's membership and congregation; one of them was a deacon, and a good one too.

But now for our journey. It was eight miles to our first appointment, and we went by water. Mrs. Scurr and the two children, with a little maid, made up our company, so that our boat was well filled. My hands, not used to rowing, soon gave out, and Brother Scurr had to do nearly all of that work. It was a hot, bright morning in the latter part of June — a lovely day — and we soon passed down the river into Lake George, and after two hours' steady pulling, made a landing opposite a log house just vacated by the settlers for one more convenient.

This was our sanctuary for the morning. Here we found a mixed company — settlers from Canada, "the States," Chippewas, etc., men, women, and children. Some of them came four, five, and eight miles; some in boats, some on foot. One old Indian was there who did not know a word of English, but sat listening as intently as if he took it all in.

After the sermon, nearly all present partook of the Lord's Supper. There were not so many there as usual; for one of the friends had just lost a little child by diphtheria, and two more lay sick; and such is the difficulty of communication that it was buried before Brother Scurr had heard of its death. This kept many away.

We now took to our boat again, and, after rowing three miles, thought we espied a beautiful place to dine; but we had reckoned without our host. Mosquitoes and their cousins, the black flies, were holding their annual camp-meeting, and about the time we landed were in the midst of a praise service. It was at once broken up on our arrival; and, without even waiting for an invitation, they joined in our repast. This was considerably shortened, under the circumstances, and we were glad to take to the water again. A word about the insect world in this region. They are very different from those farther south, being as active in the daytime as in the night. Perhaps, because of shorter seasons, they have to be at it all the time to get in their work.

Another good pull at the oar and a little help from the wind brought us to our second stage, the Indian village. On the hillside stood the schoolhouse where we were to preach. The view from this spot was lovely. Lake George lay flashing in the sunshine, and beyond the great hills stretched as far as the eye could reach, and seemed in the distance to fold one over the other, like purple clouds, until both seemed mingled into one.

We had a somewhat different audience

this time, only four white men being present; but all could understand English, except our old Indian friend of the morning, who was again present, and for whose benefit the chief's son arose after I was through, and interpreted the whole discourse, save a little part which he said he condensed as the time was short. I was both astonished and delighted. The people told me he could do so with a sermon an hour long, without a break. Most of the company, as a rule, understand both languages, and keep up a keen watch for mistakes. It is a wonderful feat. The man's gestures were perfect; he was a natural orator. I asked him if he did not find it much harder to follow some men than others. He said, "Ough! Some go big way round before they come to it; they awful hard to follow."

We took leave of our Indian friends with mingled feelings of hope as to what they might be, and of pity for what they were.

I noticed a lot of new fence-rails around the ·fields on the Canada side, and remarked that the people were industrious. "Oh, yes," said our brother; "because they burnt their fences last winter for firing." Sure enough; what is the use of a fence in winter except to burn? And then the wood is well seasoned. One church over there bought nearly all the members of the other with flour and pork; and if you ask an Indian in that region to-day to unite with your church, he says, " How much flour you give me to join?" That's business.

But it was getting late, and we had four miles' rowing yet before us. After a good hour's pull at the oars we reached the parsonage, just as the sun was setting in purple and gold behind the blue hills of Algoma. And there, as we sat watching the deepening twilight, brother Scurr told me some of the trials of missionary life in that region.

Often walking miles through the wet grass and low places, in the spring and fall, standing in his wet shoes while preaching, and then returning — in the winter on snow-shoes, following the trail (for there are no roads); in the summer, when the weather permits, by boat. When the snow was deep, and the wind was howling around his house, he had to leave his sick wife to keep his appointments miles away, and was almost afraid to enter the house on his return, for fear she had left him alone with his little ones in the wilderness. It was twelve miles to the nearest doctor on the mainland; and the only congenial companion for his wife was the missionary's wife on the Canadian side, a mile and a half away. This good sister knew something of the shady side of a missionary wife's life, as she lay for weeks hovering between life and death.

One touching little incident brother Scurr told me that deeply affected me. One dark night Deacon John Sebastian came and told him his daughter, a fine girl of some sixteen years of age, was dying, and wished to see him. The mother was a Roman Catholic; but the daughter, who attended our church with her father, had accepted Christ for her Saviour, and now desired to partake of the Lord's Supper with us ere she departed. There in the farmhouse at midnight the little company, with the mother joining, partook of the sacrament. All church distinctions were forgotten, as the Protestant father and Catholic mother sat with clasped hands, and with tear-bedimmed eyes saw their loved one go into the silent land. I left the next morning, promising to call again as soon as I could, and some time to hold meetings with them when the men were at home from fishing in the winter.

I attended the dedication of a new church at Alba costing a little over $1,000, all paid or provided for, $137 being raised on the night of dedication, in sums from two cents, given by a little girl, up to ten dollars, the highest sum given that night by one person. All our

people in the rural districts are very poor,
but often generous and self-denying. I
know of one good mother in Israel who
went without her new print dress for the
summer in order to give the dollar to
the minister at Conference. Think of
that dollar dress, my good sisters, when
you are perplexed about whether you
shall have yours cut bias, or gored, or
Mother Hubbard style, or — well, I don't
know much about styles; but "think on
these things."

XIX.

THE needs of the minute-man are as great as his field. If the army sent its minute-men to the front as poorly equipped for battle as our army of minute-men often are, it would be defeated. The man needs, besides a home, a library and good literature up to date. Religious papers a year or two old make good reading, and biographies of good men are very stimulating. A full set of Parkman's works would be of inestimable value in keeping up his courage and helping his faith. The smaller the field, the greater the need of good reading; for on the frontier you miss the society of the city, and its ministers' meetings, and the great dailies, and all the rush of modern life that is so stimulating. And yet you find men of all conditions and mental stature. A man who can get up two good sermons a week that will feed the varied types that he will meet at church needs to be a genius.

When a man has access to all the great reviews, to fine libraries, public and private, and has the stimulation that comes from constant intercourse with others, besides an income that will allow him to buy the best books, when his services begin with forty-five minutes of liturgy and song, backed with a fine pipe-organ, when he enjoys two or three months vacation into the bargain, he must be a very small specimen of a man if he cannot write a thirty-minute sermon; but when all a man's books can be put on one shelf, when his salary barely keeps the pot boiling, and he has fifty-two Sundays to fill, year in and year out, it is no wonder that short pastorates are the rule. When a man reaches his new field with no better start than many have, — the majority without a college training, and some without even a high-school education, — it

A MINUTE MAN'S PARSONAGE.

Page 196.

is not long before some of his parish will be asking a superintendent or presiding elder whether he cannot send them a good man. "Our man here," he says, "is good, but he can't preach for shucks." The new man comes, and in three months he is in the same boat. And another comes; and after a little there is as much money spent for the sustaining of these families as would keep a good man.

So it goes on, year after year. Sectarian jealousies and sectarian strivings are as bad for the spiritual development of a country as saloons. So that we find to-day, in little towns of two thousand inhabitants, ten or eleven churches, all of them little starveling things, "No one so poor to do them reverence;" while the real frontier work is left with thousands of churchless parishes.

If a man properly fitted out for his field could go at first, it would often stop the multiplication of little sects whose chief article of faith is some wretched little button-hook-and-eye or feet-washing ceremony. In the beginning, such is the weakness of the new community, a union church is inevitable, there not being enough of a kind to go around; and nothing but a lack of Christianity will break that church up.

For an example, here is a superintendent with a field a thousand miles by four hundred. He hears that a new town is started up in the mountains, a hundred and fifty miles from the railway. The stage is the only means of reaching it; no stopping on the road but twenty minutes for meals. After a tedious journey he reaches the place, and finds the usual conditions, — saloons, gambling-houses by the score, houses of every description in the process of erection.

He goes up to the hotel man, and asks whether he can procure a place for preaching. He is given the schoolhouse. He announces preaching service, and begins. The people crowd the little building; they sit or stand outside. Here are members of a dozen sects, and a solitary feet-washer feeling lonely enough. The work crowds him; and he wires to head-quarters at New York, — a strange telegram, — "For the love of God, send me a man." Just as the telegram arrives, a man who has just come from England steps into the office. He is examined, and asked whether he would like to go beyond the Rocky Mountains. He is the right stuff. "Anywhere," is the answer; and as fast as limited express can take him he hurries to the new field. He finds a great crowd outside the school-house, a revival going on, and he has hard work to reach the minister. A church is organized, and it is to be a union church. What a calamity to have the brethren living together in unity! To have Christ's prayer answered that they may be one! It's dreadful. But never mind; the Devil, in the shape of sect that holds its deformity higher than Christ, soon makes an end of that; so that the real-estate agent advertises good water, good schools, and good churches.

The only way I see out of this anti-christian warfare is to send a well-balanced, well-paid man to start with. In the case just stated, the man was a good one, and held the fort, and managed skilfully his united flock.

There are times when the best men will fail, as they do in business. The place promises great growth, and peters out; but in these small towns, where the growth will never be large, your faithful man often does a mighty work. His flock are constantly moving away, but new ones are constantly coming; and so his church is helping to fill others miles away, and it will not be until he is translated that we shall see how grand a man he was.

I remember one man with his wife and family presenting himself one day to the Superintendent of Missions. He had just left a pretty little rose-covered parsonage in England. The only place open was a very cold and hard field. The forests had been destroyed by fire. The climate was intense, either summer or winter; but he said, " I will go. I do not want to be a candidate."

And off he went with his family. In the winter his bedroom was often so cold that the thermometer registered 20° below zero; and in spite of a big stove, the temperature was at zero in mid-day near the door and windows. One of his little ones born there was carried in blankets to be baptized in the little church when it was 2° below zero. I used to send this man small sums of money that were given me by kind friends. All the money promised on this field from three churches was twenty dollars a year, and part of that paid in potatoes. The last five dollars I sent him came back. He said he felt it would not be right to take it, as he had just accepted a call to a Presbyterian church. He felt almost like making an apology for doing so, as he said, " My boys are growing up, and they can get so little schooling here that I am going to move where they can at least get an education." And then he was going to have seven hundred dollars a year. I sent the money back, saying that, as he was moving, he would probably· need it. The answer that came said he had just spent his last two cents for a postage-stamp when the five dollars came.

I suppose there are at least ten thousand minute-men on the field to-day, working under the different home missionary societies. Most of them have wives, and with their children will make an army of fifty thousand strong, the average of whose salaries will not exceed five hundred dollars per year. And on this small sum your minute-man must feed, clothe, and educate his family; and how much can he possibly use to feed his own mind? — the man who ought to be able to stand in the front ranks at all times, in order to gain the respect of the community in which he should be the leader in all good works.

XX.

THE MINUTE-MAN IN THE MINER'S CAMP.

WHEN the first minute-men went to the Pacific slope, they had a long and dangerous voyage by sea round Cape Horn; and on their arrival they had to live in a tent, pay a dollar a pound for hay, and a dollar apiece for potatoes and onions. To-day it is a very different thing to reach the mining-camps. No matter how high the mountains are, your train can climb them, doubling on itself, crossing or recrossing; or when the way is too steep, cogging its way up.

Not long since I sat in a nicely furnished room taking my dinner. My host was talking through a telephone to a man miles away, and then, with a good-by, came back to the table. I said, "That is a great contrast with your first days here." He laughed, and said, "Yes. The boats came up to where there are now great blocks of buildings; and when I preached on Sunday afternoon, I always had a bull and a bear fight to contend with around the corner. I remember one time," he said, " when the bull broke loose, and ran down the street past where I was preaching. I saw at a glance that I must close the meeting, and so pronounced the benediction; when I opened my eyes not a living soul was in sight except my wife."

At another time he approached two miners who were at work; and he told them he was building a little church, and thought they might like to help. " Yes," said one of them, " you ain't the first man that's been around here a-beggin' fer a orphan asylum. You git!" And as this was accompanied with a loaded revolver levelled at him, he obeyed. They were good men, but thought he was a gambler, as he had on a black suit. When they afterwards found out that he was all right, they helped him. Gambling in all min-

ing-camps was the common amusement.
Some little camps had scarcely anything
in sight but gambling-saloons, all licensed.

This has continued even as late as
July, 1895. The first preacher in Dead-
wood stood on a box preaching when all
around him were saloons, gambling-
houses, and worse. He was listened to
by many in spite of the turmoil all around
him, and the collection was of gold-dust.
It was accidentally spilled on the ground,
when some good-hearted miner washed it
out for him. The good man was shot
the next day as he was going over the
divide to preach in Lead City. The
miners had nothing to do with it; but
they not only got up a generous collection, but sent East and helped the man's
family.

Often a preacher has his chapel over a
saloon where the audience can hear the
sharp click of the billiard-balls, the rattle
of the dice, and the profanity of the crowd
below. One day a man who was rapidly
killing himself with drink recited in a

voice so that all in the little church could hear him : —

> " There is a spirit above,
> There is a spirit below,
> A spirit of joy,
> A spirit of woe.
> The spirit above
> Is the spirit divine,
> The spirit below
> Is the spirit of wine."

It was hard work under such circumstances to hold an audience. From the room where the man preached twelve saloons were in sight, and the audience could hear the blasting from the mines beneath them. The communion had to be held at night, as the deacons were in the mine all day. And yet those that did come were in earnest, I think. The very deviltry and awfulness of sin drove some men to a better life who under other conditions would never have gone to church. Many men were hanged for stealing horses, very few for killing a man ; while many a would-be suicide has been saved by the efforts of a true-hearted minute-man. No one but a genuine lover of his kind can do much good among the miners. In no place is a man weighed quicker. The miners are a splendid lot to work with, and none more gallant and respectful to a good woman in the world.

The free and easy style of a frontiersman is refreshing. You never hear the question as to whether the other half of your seat is engaged; although, if you are a minister in regulation dress, you will often have the seat to yourself. I remember once, when travelling in a part of the country where both lumbermen and miners abounded, a big man sat down by my side. He dropped into the seat like a bag of potatoes. After a moment's look at me, he said, " Live near here?"

" Yes, at ——."

" Umph! In business?"

" Yes; I have the biggest business in the place."

" I want to know. You ain't Wilcox?"

" I know that."

"Well, don't he own that mill?"

" Yes; but I have a bigger business than any mill."

" What are you, then ? "

" I am a home missionary."

The laugh the giant greeted this with stopped all the games and conversation in the car for a moment; but I was able to give him a good half-hour's talk, which ended by his saying, " Well, Elder, if I am ever near your place, I am coming to hear ye, sure."

I was often taken for a commercial traveller, and asked what house I was travelling for. I invariably said, " The oldest house in the country," and that we were doing a bigger business than ever. "What line of goods do you carry?" the man would ask, looking at my grip. " Wine and milk, without money and without price. Can I sell you an order ? "

At first the man would hardly believe I was a preacher. I remember talking for an hour on the boat with one young man, and after leaving him I began to read my Bible. He saw me reading, and said, "Oh! come off, now; that's too thin."

"What is the matter?" I said. "Do you mean that the paper is thin? It is; but there's nothing thin about the reading."

He at once whispered to the captain; and after the captain had answered him, he came over and apologized. "Why did you not tell me you were a minister?"

"I had no reason to," I said. "Did I say anything in my talk with you of an unchristian nature?"

"No; but I should never have known you were a minister by your clothes."

"No; and I don't propose that my tailor shall have the ministerial part of my make-up."

Time was when every trade was known by the clothes worn, and the minister is about the only one to keep his sign up. It is just as well on the frontier for him to be known by his life, his deeds, and his words. The young man above had been a wide reader; and for two hours that night under the veranda of our hotel I talked with him, and afterwards had some very interesting letters from him.

The town that same night was filled with wild revelry. It was on the eve of the Fourth of July, and newly sworn-in deputies swarmed; rockets and pistols were fired with fatal carelessness; and yet amidst it all we sat and talked, so intensely interested was the man in regard to his soul.

I close this chapter with a portion of Dr. McLean's sermon on the flowing well (he was the man our minute-man was talking with by telephone mentioned in the first part of this chapter) which will show how well it pays to place the gospel in our new settlement:—

"The first instance of which I myself happen to have had some personal observation, is of a well opened thirty years ago. Fifteen persons met in a little house, still standing, in what was then a community of less than fifteen hundred souls. They came to talk and counsel, for they were men and women in touch with God. They were considering the matter of a flowing well of the spiritual sort.

There was the valley, opportunity; and there was
the lack of sufficient religious ministration. The
moral aspect of the place could not be better sur-
mised than by the prophets word, ' Tongue faileth
for thirst.'

"They consulted and prayed, and said, ' We'll
do it!' They joined heart and hand, declaring,
'Cost what it may, we'll sink the well!' And they
did. But ah, it was a stern task. For many a day
those fifteen and the few others who joined them ate
the bread of self-denial. Delicately reared women
dismissed their household help and did the work
themselves. Enterprising, ambitious men turned
resolutely away from golden schemes, and made
their small invested capital still smaller. A few
days later on (it will be thirty years the ninth of
next December) eight men and seven women,
standing up together in a little borrowed room,
solemnly plighted their faith, and joyfully cove-
nanted to established a church of Christ of the
Pilgrim order.

"What has been the outcome of that faith and
self-denial? It has borne true Abrahamic fruit.
There stands to-day, on that foundation, a church
of more than eleven hundred members. It has
multiplied its original seventeen by more than the
hundred fold, having received to its membership
one thousand nine hundred and fifty-six souls, of
whom one-half have come upon confession. It is
a church which is teaching to-day seventeen hun-

dred in its Sunday-schools; possesses an enrolled battalion of two hundred valiant soldiers of Christian Endeavor, which maintains kindergartens and all manner of mission-industrial work ; and held the pledge, at a recent census, of thirteen hundred and twenty-two persons to total abstinence. It has a constituency of one thousand families. It reaches each week, with some form of religious ministration, two thousand five hundred persons, and has five thousand regularly looking to it for their spiritual supplies. To as many more, doubtless, does it annually furnish, in some incidental way, at least a cup of cold water in the Master's name. It is a church which has been privileged of God in its thirty years to bring forth nine more churches within the field itself originally occupied, and to lend a hand frequently with members, habitually with money in it, to four times nine new churches in fields outside its own. It is a church also, which, with no credit to itself, — for, brethren, only sink the well, pipe it, keep an open flow, and it is God who, from his bare heights and the rivers opened on them, will supply the water, — it is a church which has enjoyed the great blessedness of contributing its part to every good thing in a growing city which has grown in the thirty years from fifteen hundred to sixty thousand souls. This church, having been enabled to help on almost every good thing in its State, is recognized to-day throughout a widely extended territory as an adjunct and

auxiliary of all good things in morals, politics,
in charity, and the general humanities, — a power
for God and good in a population which, already
dense, is fast becoming one of the ganglion centres
of American civilization. It is also laying its ser-
viceable touch upon trans-oceanic continents and
intervening islands of the sea. It has furnished
ministers for the pulpit, and sent Sunday-school
superintendents and Christian workers out over a
wide area; it has consecrated already six missionaries to foreign service, and has two others under
appointment by the board; and as for wives to
missionaries and ministers, brethren, you should
just see those predatory tribes swoop down upon
its girls!

"It is a true flowing well in the midst of a valley.
Ah! those fifteen who met thirty years ago next
October made no mistake. They were within
God's artesian belt. Their divining-rod was not mis-
leading. Their call was genuine; their aim uner-
ring. They struck the vein. The flow of the rivers
breaking out from bare heights did not disappoint
them. And now behold this wide expanse of spiritual fertility! This church was not, in form, a
daughter of the American Home Missionary Society. Its name does not appear upon your family
record, and yet, in the true sense, it is your daughter.
In its infant days it sucked the breasts of churches
which had sucked yours. Its swaddling bands
you made. It was glad to get them even at

second hand. The other instance I have to quote is of but recent standing, — of not thirty years, but only three.

"On the 26th of May, three years ago, a pastor in Central California was called five hundred miles into the southern part of the State to assist in organizing a Pilgrim church. A good part of the proposing members being from his own flock. their appeal was urgent, and was acceded to. An infant organization of a few persons was brought together, and christened the Pilgrim Church of Pomona. The organization was effected in a public hall, loaned for the occasion; the church's stipulated tenure of the premises expiring at precisely 3 P. M., in order that the room might be put in order for theatrical occupancy at night. The accouchment was therefore naturally a hurried one. The constituting services had to be abbreviated. Among the things cast out was the sermon, which the visiting pastor from the north had come five hundred miles to preach. Well, sweet are the uses of adversity! Never, apparently, did loss so small gain work so great. On the lack of that initiatory sermon the Pilgrim Church of Pomona has most wonderfully thriven. The church was poor at the outset. It possessed no foot of ground, no house; only a Bible, a dozen hymn-books, and as many zealous members. Over this featherless chick was spread the brooding wing of the American Home Missionary Society. 'It was a plucky bird,' said the wisehearted pastor, already on the ground. ' Here's a case where the questionable old saw, " Half a loaf better than no bread," won't work at all. If this new well is to be driven, it must be driven to the vein. If there is to be but surface digging, let there be none. If the American Home Missionary society will supply us with six hundred dollars for the first six months, we'll make no promises, but we'll do the best we can.' Well, the G. O. S. — Grand Old Society — responded, and gave the six hundred for the desired six months. At the expiration of that period the Pilgrim Church of Pomona, located upon land and in a house of its own, bade its temporary foster-mother a grateful good-by; and, as it did so, put back into her hand two hundred of the six hundred dollars which had been given. What has been the outcome? That noble church, headed by a noble Massachusetts pastor, has become in the matter of home missions at least — but not in home missions only — the leading church of Southern California. It has to-day an enrolment of two hundred and twenty; has contributed this year three hundred and fifty dollars to your society. Alert in all activities of its own, it is a stimulus to all those of its neighbors. It had not yet got formally organized — the audacious little strutling! — before it had made a cool proposition to the handful of Pilgrim churches then existing in Southern California for the creation of a college; secured the location in its own town; itself appointed the first board of trust; and named it Pomona College. It never waited to be hatched before it began to crow; and to such purpose that it crowed up a college, which now owns two hundred acres of choice land, has a subscription-list of twenty-five thousand dollars for buildings, besides a present building costing two hundred and five thousand dollars. It has in its senior class eleven students, in its preparatory department seventy-one; and in a recent revival interest numbers a goodly group of converts; and, finally, the general association of Southern California, at its meeting within a month, committed its fifty churches fully to the subject of Christian education, to the annual presentation of the advantages and claims of Pomona College, and to an annual collection for its funds. All this, brethren, out of one of your flowing wells in three years."

XXI.

THE SABBATH ON THE FRONTIER.

WE hear a good deal of talk about the American Sabbath, so that one would think it was first introduced here ; and, indeed, the American Sabbath is our own patent. Not but what Scotland and rural England had one somewhat like it ; but the American Sabbath *par excellence* is not the Jewish Sabbath, or the European Sabbath, but the Sunday of Puritan New England, which is generally meant when we hear of the American Sabbath. But the American Sabbath of the frontier can never become the European Sabbath without getting nearer to the New England type ; for in Europe people do go to church in the morning, if they attend the beer-gardens in the afternoon. The Sabbath of the frontier has no church, and the beer-garden is open all day.

Some reader will wonder what kind of a deacon a man would make who worked on Sunday. Well, he might be better; but, remember, that for one deacon who breaks the Sabbath, there are ten thousand who break the tenth commandment, which is just as important. The fact is, you must do the best you can under the circumstances, and wait for the next generation to go up higher. It is no use finding fault with candles for the poor light and the smell of the tallow. There is only one way: you must light the gas; and it, too, must go when electricity comes. You might as well expect concrete roads, Beethoven's Symphonies, and the Paris opera, as to have all the conditions of New England life to start with under such environments. Man has greater power to accommodate himself to new conditions than the beasts that perish; nevertheless, he is subject to them, at least for a time.

I know some will be thinking of the Pilgrim Fathers, staying in the little Mayflower rather than break the Sabbath; but we must not forget, that, as a rule, the frontiers are not peopled with Pilgrim Fathers. It is true, the wildest settlers are not altogether bad ; for you could have seen on their prairie schooners within the last year these words, " In God we trusted, in Kansas we busted ; " which is much more reverent than " Pike's Peak or bust," if not quite so terse.

This is not meant for sarcasm. These words were written in a county that has been settled over two hundred and fifty years, and has not had a murderer in its jail yet, where the people talk as if they were but lately from Cornwall, where the descendants of Mayhew still live, — Mayhew, who was preaching to the Indians before the saintly Eliot.

We must remember, too, that the good men who first settled at Plymouth could do things conscientiously that your frontiersman would be shocked at. Think, too, of good John Hawkins sailing about in the ship Jesus with her .hold full of negroes, and pious New Englanders sell-ing slaves in Deerfield less than a hundred and ten years ago; of the whipping-post and the persecuting of witches; and that these good men, who would not break the Sabbath, often in their religious zeal broke human hearts. No living man respects them more than I do. You cannot sing Mrs. Hemans's words,

" The breaking waves dashed high,"

without the tears coming to these eyes; and one sight of Burial Hill buries all hard thoughts I might have about their stern rule. They were fitted for the times they lived in, and we must see to it that we do our part in our time.

In my first field I well remember being startled at a tiny girl singing out, " Hello, Elder!" and on looking up there was a batch of youngsters from the Sunday-school playing croquet on Sunday afternoon. " Hello!" said I; and I smiled and walked on. Wicked, was it not? I ought to have lectured them? Oh, yes! and lost them. Were they playing a year after? Not one of them. And, better still, the parents, who were non-church-goers, had joined the church.

The saloons and stores were open, and doing a big business, the first year; but both saloons and stores were closed, side-doors too, after that. Some of the saloon-keepers' boys, who played base-ball on Sunday, were in the Sunday-school and members of a temperance society. These saloon-keepers, and men who were not church-members, paid dollar for dollar with the Christians who sent missionary money to support the little church; and not only that, but paid into the benevo-lences of the church from five to twenty-five dollars. There is no possible way so good of getting men to be better as to get them to help in a good cause. I know men who would not take money that came from the saloon; but I did. I remembered the words, "The silver and the gold are mine," and Paul's saying, "Ask no ques-tion for conscience' sake." We might as well blame the Creator for growing the

barley because of its being put to a bad
use, as to blame a man for using the
money because it came from a bad business.   Men ought to use common sense,
even in religious things.

When a man hitches up his horse on
Sunday morning and drives fifty miles that
day and preaches four times, we admire
his zeal.   There are some who will not
blame him if he hires a livery rig, who
would condemn him if he rode on the
street-cars or railway.   I well remember
a good man, who was to speak in a church
a few miles away, saying to me, " How
shall we get there ? "   I said, " The street-
cars go right past the door."

" Oh ! I can't ride in a street-car."

" Why ?   Make you sick ? "

It never came into my head that the
man meant he could not ride on Sunday
in a street-car.

" I will tell you," said he, " what we
will do.   I will get a livery rig."

I was much amused, and bantered him,
and said, —

" I don't know about breaking the Sabbath fifty per cent. I am willing to plead limited liability with a hundred others in the street-car."

Just then a man drove up with a buggy who had been sent for us. It seemed to take a load off my friend's mind. Now, there are men who would condemn a man for this, and say he should walk; and I know men who walk ten and twelve miles on Sunday. If that is not work I do not know what is. This month I saw an article in a paper condemning the young people who had to ride on Sunday to reach their meeting. The writer would not have them travel, even in an emergency. I wonder when the Pilgrims would have reached us on that basis. It is a far cry from the Mayflower to the Lucania. Is the Sabbath greater than its Lord? I was told of one preacher who was so particular that he sent word that no appointment must be made for him that involved street-car or railway travel. So a horse was driven ten miles to fetch him, and ten miles to take him back. When the horse reached his stable that night he had travelled forty miles to keep this man from breaking the Sabbath. Who gave these brethren the right to work their horses this way, and break the Sabbath? If Moses had a man stoned to death for gathering sticks on the Sabbath, what right have you to be toasting your shins over a register that your man-servant must keep going evenly or catch it? In short, what right has any man to tamper with one of the commandments to suit himself, and place the remainder higher than love to his neighbor?

So long as the frontier Sabbath is what it is, it will be lawful to do good on the Sabbath day. Far be it from me to undervalue the Sabbath. I value it highly, but I value freedom more. The man who rides in his carriage to church has no right to condemn my riding in the street-car, and he who rides in the street-car has no right to judge the man on the train.

" Who art thou that judgest another man's servant?" " One man esteemeth one day above another; another esteemeth every day alike. Let every man be fully persuaded in his own mind." " Stand fast, therefore, in the liberty wherewith Christ hath made us free, and be not entangled again with the yoke of bondage."

XXII.

THE FRONTIER OF THE SOUTH-WEST.

THE South-west is different from all other parts of the country. The Anglo-Saxon is everywhere else in the ascendant. Here the Latin races are dominant. It is astonishing to find so many oldest churches all over the country. The superlative is a national trait. We have either the oldest or the youngest, the greatest or the smallest, or the only thing in the world. However, it is almost certain that the oldest church and house are to be found in Santa Fé. The Church of San Miguel was built seventy years before the landing of the Pilgrims, and the house next to the church fifty years. It is the oldest settled, is the farthest behind, has the most church-members per capita, and is the most ignorant and superstitious part of the land. In one part Mormonism holds

OLDEST HOUSE IN THE UNITED STATES, SANTA FÉ, NEW MEXICO.

Page 220.

sway. In the other, Roman Catholicism of two centuries ago is still the prevailing religion.

It is a curious fact; but in this latter respect the North-east and the South-west almost join hands; for Lower Canada sent us Old France, and the South-west remains Old Spain. Here, as a man travels through Western Texas, New Mexico, and Arizona, only his Pullman car, and especially his Pullman porter, makes him realize that he is in America. In the eastern part of Texas the buzzards fill the air as they are hovering over the dead cattle. In the western part the dead cattle dry up and are blown away. Meat keeps indefinitely. There are no flies there, few insects, and the flowers are almost odorless, perhaps on account of the lack of insect-life. The very butcher-signs look strange. Instead of the fat, meek ox on a sign, we have a mad bull charging a Spanish matador.

Here comes a Mexican with a fifty-dollar hat on his head, and fifty cents would almost buy the rest of his clothes. He marches by with the strut of a drum-major. The best streets and the finest houses are often not homes. The plains look as if they would not keep a cow alive ; and yet here in the South-west we find some of the finest grazing-lands in the world, although it takes twenty-five acres to feed a cow. But what of that? the acres are unlimited. The black-tailed antelope are seen running from your train; while the prairie-dog sits, like all small things, barking impudently, or, with a few electric twists of his little tail he dives below, where a rattlesnake and an owl keep his house in order, i.e., keep the population down so that the progeny would not kill all the grass, and so starve at last; with himself would go the cattle; so the economy of nature keeps up its reputation everywhere. As some have said, when salmon are scarce hens' eggs become dear; for the otter takes to the land and kills the rabbits, and the weasel, finding his stores low, visits the hen-coops — and up goes the price of eggs.

The minute-man in the South-west has a big field. He is often hundreds of miles from his next church. He preaches to the cowboys one day, to the Digger Indians or the blanket variety the next. He is off among the miners, and sometimes in less than four hours he must change from the cold mountain air to the heat which requires two roofs to the house in order to keep it cool enough. He eats steak that has come one thousand miles from the East, although ten thousand cattle are all about him. He passes a million cows, and yet has to use condensed milk for his coffee or go without.

He finds himself in the midst of the grandest scenery on the continent. In his long journey he often finds himself sleeping on the plain outside the teepees of his red brother, rather risking the tarantulas, lizards, and rattlers that may come, than the thousands of smaller nuisances that are sure to come if he goes under cover. He is in the midst of a past age; and as he visits the pueblos, he would not be surprised to see De Soto come forth, so Spanish are his surroundings. The adobe building prevails everywhere, cool in summer, warm in winter, and in this climate well nigh indestructible.

The priesthood are centuries removed from those of the East. Here he will meet with men living in the Middle Ages, beating their backs with cactus until the blood streams, and often dying under self-inflicted blows. We often hear of America having no ruins, no ancient history. This may be so in regard to time; but in regard to conditions we are in the time of Boadicea of the ancient Briton, and in the South-west are ruins of buildings that were inhabited when William was crowned at Westminster. So great are the States of the South-west that the counties are larger than New England States; and you may be stuck in a blizzard in northern Texas, while people in the southern portion are eating oranges out-doors with the oleanders for shade-trees.

I will close this chapter with a description given me in part by the Rev. E. Lyman Hood, who was Superintendent of Missions in the South-west until he was broken down by his arduous toil.

One evening he found himself at the opening of an immense cañon, on the lofty tops of which the snow was perpetual. Sheltered beneath its mighty walls, flowers of semi-tropical luxuriance flourished, and birds of gorgeous plumage flitted here and there; while humming-birds, like balls of metal, darted among the flowers. A little silver streamlet ran down the cañon until lost in the blue distance; and here our minute-man stood lost in reverent admiration. The sun was going down in pomp of purple and gold; and the little stream changed its colors with the clouds, until in a moment it became black; a cold wind came down the cañon, the flowers closed their petals, and with a twitter here and there the birds went to roost. And then our minute-man looked up aloft, where the sun still gilded the great cañon's shoulders until they glowed

like molten metal, and kissed the forehead
of an Indian who stood like a statue waiting the sun's setting. Another moment
and it was gone, and our Indian stood like
a silhouette against the sky, when he at
once wheeled toward the east, and, stoop-
ing, lit a fire; then drawing his ragged
blanket around him, prepared to watch
all night until the sun came up in the eastern horizon, watching for the return of his
Saviour Montezuma. And thus far he has
watched in vain.

A strange fact, — a poor tribe still waiting and watching for a Saviour in a land
where there are over twenty million church-
members, some of whom ride past him in
their palace-cars to take a palatial steamer,
and travel thousands of miles to find a soul
to save. Over twelve denominations striving in Mexico to win souls, and scarcely a
thing done for the hundreds of thousands
of Mexicans in our own land, and over
forty tribes of Indians. And all this in the
year of our Lord 1895.

XXIII.

DARK PLACES OF THE INTERIOR.

I want to picture out in this chapter one of the hardest fields the minute-man has to labor in. I think there are greater inequalities to be found in our land than in any other, at least a greater variety of social conditions. Times have changed much in the last twenty-five years. The consolidating of great business concerns has made a wide gulf between the employer and employee such as never before existed outside of slavery.

It is not true to say that the rich are growing richer, and the poor poorer; for the poor could not be poorer. There never was a time when men were not at starvation-point in some places. We have to-day thousands of men who never saw the owner of the property that they work upon. There is a fearful distance between the gentlemen and ladies in their four-in-hand turnout and the begrimed men who come up into the daylight out of our great coal-mines, or those who handle the heavy iron ore. I have seen men whose hands could be pared like a horse's hoof without drawing the blood, who were going back to Germany to stay, — men who had been lured over by the promise of big wages, who, as they said, averaged "feefty cent a day." I have seen sixty and seventy men living in a big hut, with two or three women cooking their vegetables in a great iron kettle, and dipping them out with tin ladles. I have seen little boys by the score working for a few cents a day, and four, five, and seven families living in one house, and where all the pay was store-pay, and did not average five dollars a week, and where it was not safe to walk at night, and murder was common, — and you could find within a few miles cities where there were men who would say that the whole of the above was a lie.

When I first talked on these regions, I could think of nothing else; and some good men advised me not to tell of what I had seen. It smacked too much of social-ism, they said. I remarked, " You will hear of starving, bloodshed, and riot from that region before long." And so they did. The State troops were called out more than once. And here in the midst of this misery our minute-man went. Before the mines were opened, a little stream of clear water flowed between green banks and through flowery meads; cattle dotted the meadows, and peaceful farm-houses nestled under the trees. But all this was soon changed. The green sod was turned up, the clear stream became a muddy, discolored torrent, and wretched little houses took the place of the farm-houses. Low saloons abounded. Our minute-man was warned that his life would be in danger. On the other hand, he was offered three times the salary he was getting as a missionary if he would become a foreman. But the man is one of the last of that noble army of pioneers that count not their life dear.

When our man tried to find a place to preach, there was none save an old dilapidated schoolhouse. The window-sashes were broken, the panels of the door gone. The place was beyond a little stream, which had to be crossed upon a log. It was nearly dark before his audience arrived. The women, much as they wanted to go, were ashamed of the daylight. Many of the young girls had on but one garment. The men were a rough-looking lot. The place was lighted with candles in lanterns, the flames of which fluttered with the draughts, and gutters of tallow ran down. What a contrast to the church a few miles away, where the seats were cushioned, and a quartet choir sang, "The Earth is the Lord's," with a magnificent organ accompaniment! What a gulf between these poor souls and those who came in late, not because of poor clothes, but because of fine ones! And yet I suppose they did not perceive it, perhaps they did not know. But it does seem to me that when men hear that " The Earth is the Lord's," it ought to make them think how small a proportion of earth they will make when mingled with the dust from which they came.

But to return to our meeting. Our man is not from the colleges, but is a rare man (don't misunderstand me. Nothing is so much needed to-day as well-educated men ; and I am not one of those who think that it spoils a razor to sharpen it) ; and he has not spoken long before the tears fall fast, and many a poor fellow who once sang the songs of Zion comes home to his Father's house. Still, they tell our man it is not safe for him to come ; but he does ; and under great difficulties he builds a church and parsonage. And then he tries to have a reading-room. Naturally he thinks that the man who is making so much money out of the earth will help him. He offers twenty-five dollars, which our minute-man spurns. He is going to give double that out of his meagre salary, and tells the man so ; but the man's excuse is that he pays four hundred dollars a year towards the church music. Think of that. And he pays to hear that " The Earth is the Lord's," and still does not hear. The little room is built and furnished without his help, and saves many a poor fellow from drink.

Our man has several other places to preach in, each worse than the other. In one town it is on Sunday afternoon, but he has to wait for the room until the dance is over. In another town he builds a church ; and to this day may be seen the bullet-holes near the pulpit, where men have shot at him, hoping to kill their best friend. As he is passing along the street one day with a companion, a man runs across the road from a saloon, plunges a knife into the heart of the man who is walking with our minute-man, and he drops dead in his tracks. Amid such scenes as this our hero still works. He has been the means of stopping more than one strike ; and one would think that the rich companies would at least give more than they do to help these men at the front, who would make Pinkerton's men and State troops unnecessary.

In the meantime the men are here. Can we expect that these men, coming from their huts on the Danube,— seeing our fine houses, the American working-men's children well clothed and attending school,— are going to be content? Do we want them to be? The worst thing that could happen to them and ourselves would be for them to be content with their present condition. No greater danger could menace the Republic than thousands of Europeans coming here to live, and remaining in their present condition. We condemn them for coming and underworking our men ; and we condemn them when they want more, and are bound to get it.

Many say, " Keep them out." But there are several things in the way. Rich corporations, mine-owners, and railways are bound to get them. And would you keep the men from·which we sprung in overcrowded Europe, while we have a continent with but seventy millions? Is there any real love in that which sends a missionary to Europe to save souls on the Don, that will not let their bodies live on the Hudson? Do we believe that "The Earth is the Lord's"? Let me close this chapter with a quotation from Roger Williams's letter to the Town of Providence:—

"I have only one motion and petition which I earnestly pray the town to lay to heart, as ever they look for a blessing from God on the town, in your families, your corn and cattle, and your children after you. It is this, that after you have got over the black brook of some soul bondage yourselves, you tear not down the bridge after you, by leaving no small pittance for distressed souls that come after you."

XXIV.

THE DANGEROUS NATIVE CLASSES.

WE hear much about the dangerous
foreigners that come to us, but little about
the dangerous native. There is not a
type, whether of poverty or ignorance,
but what we can match it. Leaving out
the negro, we have over ninety per cent
Anglo-Saxon in the South. Here we find
a strange lot of paradoxes, — the most
American, the most ignorant, the most
religious, the most superstitious, and the
most lawless. Take the lowest class of
Crackers, and we have the whole of the
above combined, with millions of mountain whites to match. Yet in this same
South land are the most gentlemanly, and
the most lady-like, and the most hospit-
able people in the country. The Cracker
classes are descendants of the English,
but what kind of English? The offscour-

ings of prison and dockyards, sent over to work on the plantations before slave labor was introduced.

The mountain whites are the descendants of the Scotch-Irish. As many people seem to think this means a Scotch parent on one side and an Irish upon the other, it may be well to state that the Scotch-Irish are the descendants of Scotch people who immigrated to Ireland. But it ought not to be forgotten that the mountain whites are the descendants of Scotch-Irish of two centuries ago, a very different people from the Scotch-Irish of to-day. Here in the mountains we find some three millions, often without schools, and waiting sometimes for years for a funeral sermon after the person has been buried. Towns can be found over seventy years old organized with a court-house and no church.

"Yes," they say, "the Methodists started one some years ago; but the Baptists threw the timber into the Cumberland, and sence then we ain't had no church."

Here one of our minute-men had two horses shot under him, and another missionary was nearly killed.

Here you may find families of twenty and more, living in a wretchedly constructed house, on bacon and corn-meal, hoe-cakes, and dodgers. I started once to stay over night in one of these houses. As we came near to the place, I found that my host was a school-teacher. He had taught twenty-two schools. He meant by this that he had taught that many years. The kitchen was as black as smoke could make it; the butter was stringy, caused by the cows eating cotton-seed; and my seat a plank worn smooth by use, with legs which stuck up through it, which would have been better had they been worn more. I suppose in some way I involuntarily showed my feelings; for the woman noticed it, and said, "Yer oughter put up with one night what we uns have ter all the time."

I said "That's the trouble; I could when I got used to it."

The room I slept in had a hole in the end that you could drive a span of horses through. It had been left for a chimney. As I found out that the day before a rattlesnake had come into the house, and the good woman had to defend herself with the fire-poker, I did not sleep so well as I might. The possibility of a rattler in the dark, and no poker handy, filled me with uneasy thoughts; but as people get up with the sun, the time passed, and I was glad to get back to civilized life.

I noticed that the cotton was ridged up with concave rows of earth, which was covered with rank weeds. This was done to keep the water from running off too quickly. I asked whether sage would not hold the ridges as good as weeds. "Oh, yes!" they said, and it brought a dollar a pound; but they had never thought of that.

Some of the States do not have seventy school-days in the year; and the whole South to-day has not as many public libraries as the State of Massachusetts. A man needs perfect health to enjoy some of the pastoral work which he must do if he intends making a success among the mountain whites. One thing should never be forgotten. The poor whites of the mountains were loyal to the Union, and out from this type came the greatest American we have had, Abraham Lincoln.

Here, then, is plenty of material to work on, — families big enough to start a small church, and who do not send to England for pug-dogs for lack of progeny. Here is the rich fields, and here must the race be lifted before the millions of blacks can have a chance. Education must be pushed; and then will come a period of scepticism, for this people are fifty years behind the times.

Several people were sitting on a large veranda; and one man, a preacher lately from Texas, was telling us of his visit. Among other things he spoke of the cyclone-pits, and said, "Seems to me, brother, a man can't have much faith in

God who would go into a pit. I would not; would you?"

"No," replied mine host. "Men seem to me to be losing faith. I once raised a woman up by prayer that three doctors had given up. Aunt Sally, have ye any of that liver invigorator? I kind of feel as if I needed some."

Here was a man who had prayed a woman out of the jaws of death, calling for liver medicine. None of them seemed to see the incongruity of it. One good old deacon that I knew horrified his pastor, who was a strong temperance man, by furnishing the communion with rye whiskey. The old·man meant all right; but he had neglected to replenish the wine, and thought something of a spirituous nature was needed, and so brought the whiskey.

It is a fact worth noting, that we have to-day, in the year 1895, millions of men living in conditions as primitive as those of the eighteenth century, while in the same land we are building houses which are lighted and heated with electricity; that some men worship in houses built of logs, without glass windows, and others worship in buildings that cost millions; that in the former case men have lived in this way for over two hundred years, and the latter less than fifty since the Indian's tepee was the only dwelling in sight; that to-day may be seen the prairie schooner drawn by horses, oxen, or mules, and in one case a horse, a cow, and a mule, the little shanty on wheels, the man sitting in the doorway driving, and his wife cooking the dinner. But so it is. We have all the varieties of habitation, from the dugout of the prairie to the half-million summer cottage at Bar Harbor; and from a single Indian pony, we have all kinds of locomotion, up to the vestibuled palace on wheels.

That I may not seem to be over stating the condition of the mountain whites, and the dangers among our own people, I close with a quotation from Dr. Smart's Saratoga address:—

" Let me tell you of just one experiment of letting a people alone, and its result. Shall we trust that American institutions and American ideas, that the press and schools, will ultimately Americanize them? In the eastern part of Kentucky, in the western part of North Carolina and West Virginia, there is a section of country about the size of New Hampshire and New York, — one of the darkest spots on the map of the South. The people living there have been there for over a hundred years, and are of Scotch-Irish extraction. Whole counties can be found in which there is not a single wagon-road. Most of the houses are of one story, without a window, or only a small one ; and the door has to be kept open to let in the light. I have it from good authority that when the first schoolmistress went there to teach, she stipulated that she should have a room with a window in it, and a lock to the door. Very few of the people can read or write. They have no newspapers, no modern appliances for agriculture, no connection with the world outside and around them. This is the land of the ' moonshiner.' They love whiskey, and so they manufacture it. The pistol and bowie-knife are judge and sheriff. Bloodshed is common, and barbarism a normal state of society. These men were not slaveholders in the times before the war. They were as loyal to the Union as any others who fought for the old flag, and they served in the Union army when they got a chance.

When Bishop Smith in a large and influential meeting spoke of them, he touched the Southern and Kentucky pride, especially when he pointed out what a moral and spiritual blot they were upon the South. Now, why are they there a hundred years behind us in every respect? Why are they sunk so low? Simply because they have been let alone. They are just as much separated from this land, without any share in its marvellous progress, as if a Chinese wall had been built around them. They have been let alone; and American institutions, American schools, and the American press, have flowed around them and beyond them without effect."

XXV.

CHRISTIAN WORK IN THE LUMBER-TOWN.

UNTIL a few years ago I knew little or nothing of mill-towns or lumber-camps. I had seen a saw-mill that cut its thousand feet a day when running, and it was generally connected with some farm through which ran a stream. It was a very innocent affair. But in 1889 I saw for the first time the great forests of pine, and became acquainted with part of the immense army of lumbermen. Michigan alone had at that time some forty thousand; Wisconsin has as many; Georgia, Alabama, and Louisiana are now engaged in a vast work; and when we add the great States of Oregon and Washington, with their almost illimitable forests, we feel that we are speaking within bounds when we say an immense army.

The one great difficulty of the problem is the transitory character of the work — like Count Rumford's stoves, if they could only have been patented and money made out of them, every house would use them ; so if the lumber village had come to stay, many a church would have gone in and built. But more than once a man in authority has said, " Oh, I have looked that field over, and it won't amount to much." No one who has not had experience in the field can form any adequate idea of its vastness or its crying needs. The one great trouble of the whole question is the massing of so many men away from the softening influence of wife and mother. It is unnatural ; and nature's laws, as sacred as the Decalogue, are broken in unnatural crimes, and sins unknown to the common run of men.

The lumber business may be divided into three distinct classes of workers, — the mill-men, the camp-men, and the river-men. The last are the smallest company, but the hardest to reach. They flit from stream to river, from the river to the lake, from scenes of sylvan beauty to the low groggery — and worse. Their temporary home is often made of blackened logs papered with *Police Gazettes*, which come in vast numbers, and form the largest part of their not very select reading. Books of the Zola type, but without their literary excellence, are legion. Good books and good literature would be a boon in these camps.

To give you an idea of the rapid march of the lumber-camp, come with me into the primeval forest. It is a winter day. The snow is deep, and the lordly pines are dressed like brides in purest white; one would think, to look at their pendent branches, that Praxiteles and all his pupils had worked for a century in sculpturing these lovely forms. Not a sound is heard save our sleigh-bells, or some chattering squirrel that leaps lightly over the powdery snow; a gun fired would bring down a harmless avalanche. It is a sight of unsurpassed beauty in nature's privacy; but alas, how soon the change!

An army of brawny men invade the lovely scene. Rude houses of logs are quickly erected; and men with axe and saw soon change the view, and with peavey and cant-hook the logs are loaded and off for the rollway. Inside the largest house are bunks, one above another; two huge stoves with great iron cylinders, one at each end, give warmth; while in picturesque confusion, socks and red mackinaws and shirts hang steaming by the dozens. There is a cockloft, where the men write their letters, and rude benches, where they sit and smoke and tell yarns till bedtime. In a few weeks at the farthest the grand old forest is a wreck; a few scrubby oaks or dwindling beech-trees are all that are left. The buildings rot down, the roofs tumble in, and a few camp-stragglers trying to get a living out of the stumpy ground are all that are left; and solitude reigns supreme.

On stormy days hundreds of the men

go into the nearest village, and sin revels in excess. In many a small town, mothers call their little ones in from the streets, which are soon full of men drunken and swearing, ready for fight or worse. At such times they hold the village in a reign of terror, and often commit crimes of a shocking nature, and no officer dares molest them. A stranger coming at such a time would need to conduct himself very discreetly or he would get into trouble. A volume might be filled with the outrageous things done in these small lumber-towns. Ireland is not the only place that suffers from absentee landlords.

The condition of the children is pitiable, brought up in an atmosphere of drunkenness and debauchery; swearing as natural as breathing; houses packed so closely that you can reach across from one window to another. The refuse is often emptied between the houses; diseases of all kinds flourish, and death is ever busy. Eight or ten nationalities are often found in these towns, — men who cannot spell their names, and men who went to St. Paul's and admired Canon Liddon, or New York men that went to Beecher's church.

Here a house which cost less than a hundred dollars, and inside of it an organ costing one hundred and twenty-five dollars, and a forty-dollar encyclopædia. The next house is divided by stalls like a stable, with bed in one, stove in another, and kitchen in the third. With a population as mixed as this, and in constant flux, what, you ask, can the church do? I answer, much, very much, if you can only get a church there; but when the church which gives much more than any other gives but a quarter of a cent per day per member, is it any wonder that hundreds of churchless lumber-towns call in vain for help from the sanctuary? Some small villages can be found where every family is living in unlawful relations.

Now, remember this, the lumberman is made of the same clay that we are, and it is his environment that brings to the front the worst that is in him. He is reached by practical Christianity as easily as any other man. The shame and reproach belong to us for neglecting him, and there is no other way that we so dishonor him whom we call Master as to say his commands are not practicable. Is it asking too much from the rich men who get their money by the toil of these men, that out of their millions they should spend thousands for the moral welfare of those who make them rich? And yet too often they do not even know their own foremen, and in many cases have never visited the property they own.

I once asked a rich lumber-man for a subscription for missions, saying I was sorry he was not at the church when I took up my collection. "Jinks! I am glad I was not there," he said; "I gave away ten dollars Saturday night."

Now, this man had been cutting off from his land for thirty years, and had just sold a quarter of a million dollars' worth of it, and still had land left. But on the other hand, be it known that the men in these villages who make no profession of religion actually give dollar for dollar with the Christian church-members to sustain the frontier churches. Saloon-keepers, and often Roman Catholics, help to support the missionary church.

The mission churches of the lumber regions are like springs in the desert, but for which the traveller would die on his way; and thousands of church-members scattered from ocean to ocean were born of the Spirit in some one of these little churches that did brave work in a transient town.

To do work in these places aright, one must drop all denominational nonsense, — be as ready to pray and work with the dying Roman Catholic as with a member of his own church, and do as I did, — lend the church building to the priest, because disease in the town would not permit of using the private houses at the time, and so help to fill up the gap between us and the old mother that nursed us a thousand years.

In every new town, in every camp, should be a standing notice, "No cranks need apply."

Here is a brawny man who does not like the church. He hates the name of preacher, and threatens that he had better not call at his house. Scarlet fever takes his children down. The despised preacher, armed with a basket of good things, raps at the door. Pat opens it. "Good-morning, Pat. I heard your little ones were sick, and my wife thought your wife would have her hands full, and she has sent a few little things — not much, but they will help a little, I hope."

The tears are in Pat's eyes. "Come in, Elder, if you are not afraid, for we have scarlet fever here."

"That is the very reason I came, my boy;" and Pat is won. The very man that swore the hardest because the elder was near, now says, "Don't swear, boys; there's the elder."

Yes; and when men have heard that the new preacher has helped in the house stricken with small-pox or typhoid, he has the freedom of the village, or the camp, and is respected. And so the village missionary does some good in the mill-town. But what is one man among so many? See this little place with less than five hundred population. Two thousand men come there for their mail, and the average distance to the next church is over twenty miles; and one man is totally inadequate to the great work before him.

These villages and camps ought to have good libraries, a hall well lighted, inno-cent amusements, lectures, and entertain-ments, and in addition to this, an army of men carrying good books and visiting all the camps; and there is nothing to hinder but the lack of money, and the lack of will to use it in those who have abundance. I lately passed through a lumber-town of seven ·thousand inhabi-tants. Four or five millionnaires lived there. One had put up an $80,000 training-school, another a memorial building costing $160,000. This is the other extreme. But up to date the lumber-regions have been shamefully neglected, and thousands of boys and girls are growing up to drift to our great cities and form the dangerous classes, fitted for it by their training. It is better to clear the water-sheds than to buy filters, and the cheapest policeman of the city is the missionary in the waste places of our land.

XXVI.

TWO KINDS OF FRONTIER.

SOME years ago it is said that a man lost his pig, and in searching for it he found it by hearing its squealing. The pig had fallen in a hole; and in getting it out, the man saw the rich copper ore which led to the opening of the Calumet and Hecla mines, and more recently the Tamarack. More ore per ton goes into the lake from the washing than comes out of most mines. So rich is this ore that very few fine mineral specimens are found in the mines. Millions of money have been expended in developing them, and millions more have come out of them.

With such richness one would expect to find the usual deviltry that abounds in mining regions ; but such is not the case. In the early days, the mines were worked on Sunday in the Keweenaw region; but through the resolute stand of two Scotchmen, who would not work on Sunday, the work was stopped on Saturday night at twelve o'clock, and resumed again Monday at twelve A.M. And this was found to be a benefit all round, as it generally is. I knew of a salt-well where the man thought it must be kept going all the time; but one Sunday he let it rest, and found that, instead of coming up in little spits, it accumulated, so that, as he said, it came "ker-plump, ker-plump."

When the little church was first started in Calumet, the projectors of it were asked how much money they would want from the society to help them. The answer was, a check for two hundred dollars for home missions. Knowing this, I was not surprised to find good churches, good schools, good society, a good hotel, and as good morals as you can find anywhere. Not a drop of liquor is sold in Calumet. This shows what may be done by starting right; and there is no occasion for a mining-camp to be any worse except through criminal neglect of the owners.

We pass on to the new mines farther west, and what do we find? Saloons packed twenty in a block, dance-houses with the most degrading attachments, scores of young lives sacrificed to man's lust, the streets dangerous after dark, and not pleasant to be on at any time. The local newspaper thus heralded a dog-fight at the theatre, "As both dogs are in good condition, it will prove one of the most interesting fights ever seen on this range."

Here is the copy of an advertisement: "At the Alhambra Theatre. Prize-fight, thirty rounds or more. Prize, $200,00. Don't mistake this for a hippodrome. Men in fine condition. Plucky. Usual price."

Here is another: "Saturday, Sunday, and Monday, balloon ascension. A lady from the East will go up hanging by her toes. At a great height she will drop deeds of lots, the lucky possessor only to write his or her name to own the lot. Persons coming from a distance, and buying lots, will have railroad money refunded Men leaving work, and buying, their wages paid. Everybody come and have a good time. Remember the date's Saturday, Sunday, and Monday."

Here pandemonium reigned. What a place to raise a family! Thousands of little children were growing up under these awful conditions. I have gone up the lake more than once when innocent young girls were on the boat, expecting to find places at the hotel, only to meet with temptation and ruin; some committing suicide, some becoming more reckless than the brutes that duped them.

The harbor could be reached only by daylight, and with vessels of light draft; and no sooner were they unloaded than they steamed off again, not to return for a week. Thus there was no way for these unfortunate girls to get back if they wished, for it was a dense forest for thirty miles to the nearest railway point, in the meanwhile, worse than death came to those who fell into the clutches of such fiends in human shape.

One man, the chief owner there, threatened the bold rascals; but they said they would build their house upon a raft and defy him. He said, "I will cut you loose." They snapped their fingers at him, burnt his hotel, and shot him. Did this go on in the dark? No; the Chicago and Minneapolis and St. Paul's newspapers wrote it up. I spoke of it until warned I must not tell such awful things: it would be too shocking.

Into such awful places our minuteman goes, and takes his family too. It is hard work at first, but little by little sin must give way before righteousness. It is strange that Christian men and women can draw incomes from these mines, and feel no duty towards the poor men who work for them. I met one such man upon the steamer coming from Europe. He had been over twice that season. He had made his thousands, and was going back with his family to travel in Egypt, and leave his children with their nurses at Cairo.

He admitted everything I told him about the condition of things on his own property; and in answer as to whether he would help, said, "No; it's none of my funeral." How any man could walk those streets, and see fair young girls drunk at nine A.M., and in company with some of the worst characters that ever disgraced humanity, and not feel his obligations to his Lord and fellow-man, is more than I can understand.

The awful cheapness of human life, the grim jokes upon the most solemn things, could only be matched in the French Revolution. I saw in one store, devoted to furniture and picture-frames, a deep frame with a glass front, and inside a knotted rope, and written underneath, " Deputy-sheriff's necktie, worn by —— for murdering Mollie ——" on such a date. This was for the sheriff's parlor.

Hard times have made a great change since I walked those streets. The roar of traffic has given place to the howl of hungry wolves that have prowled among the deserted shanties in midday in search of food; and the State has had to supply food and clothing to the poor, while my man, who had made his thousands, was studying the cuneiform inscription, in Egypt. It ought to make him think, when he sees the mummies of dead kings being shipped to England to raise turnips, that some day he will have a funeral all his own.

XXVII.

BREAKING NEW GROUND.

" This is the forest primeval."

A GRAND sight is the forest primeval
when the birds fill all its arches with song,
or we sweep through them to the music
of sleigh-bells. A pleasant sight is the
farmer, surrounded by his wife and children, with well-kept farm, ample barns,
and well-fed stock. But what wild desola-
tion once reigned where now these fine
farms are seen! The great trees stretched
on for hundreds of miles. The hardy settler came with axe and saw and slow-paced
oxen, cleared a little space, and built a
log hut. For a little time all goes well;
then · thistles, burdocks, mulleins, and
briers come to pester him and increase his
labors. Between the blackened log-heaps
fire-weeds spring up. The man and his
wife grow old fast. Ague shakes their

BREAKING NEW GROUND.

confidence as well as their bodies. Schools are few, the roads mere trails.

Then a village starts. First a country store; then a saloon begins to make its pestilential influence felt. The dance thrives. The children grow up strong, rough, ignorant. The justice of the peace marries them. No minister comes. The hearts once tender and homesick, in the forest grow cold and hardened. At funerals perhaps a godly woman offers prayer. Papers are few and poor. Books are very scarce. In winter the man is far off, with his older boys, in the lumber-camps, earning money to buy seed, and supplies for present wants. The woman pines in her lonely home. The man breaks down prematurely. Too many of these pioneers end their days in insane asylums. It is the third generation which lives comfortably on pleasant farms, or strangers reap that whereon they bestowed no labor.

This may seem too dark a picture. Song and story have gilded the pioneer life so that its realities are myths to most people. It is better when a colony starts with money, horses, books, etc. ; but it is hard enough then. Few keep their piety. I visited a community where nearly every family were church-members in their early homes ; but, after twenty years, only one family had kept up the fire upon the altar. It is hard to break up such fallows. How different had a minister gone with them, and a church been built!

The missionary has different material altogether to work on in the natural born pioneer. I visited one family which had a black bear, two hounds, some pet squirrels, cats, and a canary ; over the fireplace hung rifles, deer-horns, and other trophies of the chase. The man was getting ready to move. At first his nearest neighbors were bears and deer ; but now a railway had come, also schools and churches. He said, " 'Tain't like it was at fust ; times is hard ; have to go miles for a deer ; folks is getting stuck up, wearing biled shirts, getting spring beds and rockers, and then ye can't do nothin' but some one is making a fuss. I shall cl'ar out of this!"

And he did, burying himself and family in the depths of the woods. The homesteader often takes these deserted places, after paying a mere trifle for the improvements.

Homesteaders are numerous, generally very poor, and are apt to have large families. One man, who had eight hundred dollars, was looked upon as a Rothschild. Many families had to leave part of their furniture on the dock, as a pledge of payment for their passage or freight-bill. But, homesteaders or colonists, all must work hard, be strong, live on plain fare, and dress in coarse clothing. The missionary among these people must do the same. A good brother told me that, on a memorable cold New Year's Day, he went into the woods to cut stove-wood, taking for his dinner a large piece of dry bread. By noon it was frozen solid; but, said he, " I had good teeth, and it tasted sweet."

Another lived without bread for some time, being thankful for corn-meal. Those who live far from the railways are often brought to great straits, through stress of weather and the wretched roads. Little can be raised at first; the work must be done in a primitive way.

As it is with the farmer, so it is with the missionary. The breaking of new ground is hard work. Everything at first seems delightful. The people are glad, " seeing they have a Levite for their priest." They promise well. The minister starts in with a brave heart, and commences to underbrush and cut down the giant sins that have grown on such fat soil. But as they come down, he, too, finds the thistles and mulleins; jealousies, sectarian and otherwise, come in and hinder him, and it is a long, weary way to the well-filled church, the thriving Sunday-school, and the snug parsonage.

Often he fares like the early farmer. The pioneer preacher is seldom seen in the pretty church, but a man of a later generation. The old man is alive yet, and perhaps his good wife ; but they are plain folks, and belong to another day. Sometimes they look back with regret to the very hardships they endured, now transfigured and glorified through the mists of years. Should the reader think the picture too dark, here are two condensed illustrations from Dr. Leach's " History of Grand Traverse Region." Remember, this was only a few years ago, and where to-day seventy thousand people dwell, on improved farms, and in villages alive with business, having all the comforts, and not a few of the luxuries, of civilized life.

In those early days, Mr. Limblin, finding he had but one bushel and a half of corn left, and one dollar and a half in money, prevailed on a Mr. Clark to take both corn and money to Traverse City, thirty miles away, and get groceries with the money, and have the corn ground, Mr. Clark to have half for the work. One ox was all the beast of burden they had.

Mr. Clark started with the corn on the back of the ox; about half-way he exchanged for a pony and sled for the rest of the road, leaving the ox with the Indians till his return. On his way back, a fierce snowstorm hid the shores of the bay from view. Presently he came to a wide crack in the ice; his pony, being urged, made a spring, but only got his fore hoofs on the other side. Mr. Clark sprang over and grasped the pony's ears, but, as he pulled, his feet slipped, and down he came. His cries brought the Indians, who rescued him and the pony. Exhausted, he crawled back to their camp. But, alas! the corn-meal and groceries were at the bottom of the bay. A sad scene it was to see his poor wife's tears on his arrival home.

Rev. Peter Daugherty, now of Wisconsin, was the first missionary in these parts. He once missed his way; and night coming on, he saw that he must sleep in the woods. The air was chill. Not daring to build a fire for fear of the damage it might do to the dry woods, he cast about for a shelter. Spying two headless barrels on the beach, with much trouble he crawled into them, drawing them as close together as he could, and so passed the night. He got up very early and finished his journey. But do we have such places yet? and does the missionary still have to expose himself? Yes, friends, there are scores of such places in every frontier State and Territory; and strong men are needed more than ever to break up new ground, and cause the desert and solitary places to be glad and blossom as the rose. Send us such men!

XXVIII.

SOWING THE SEED.

THE land is bound to grow its crop. The more the land has been enriched, the greater will be that crop, of useful grain or rank weeds. And the only way to keep the weeds from gaining the victory is by sowing good seed and pulling the weeds. A friend in Detroit once called my attention to the luxuriant weeds in a fenced lot we were walking by. In the vacant lot close by, the weeds were stunted. In the fenced lot a market gardener once lived. He had enriched the soil.

Our country is to have a rank growth of something. Rich in the blood of many nationalities, with freedom well-nigh to license, what will the harvest be if left without spiritual husbandry? Dr. Mulhall's " Dictionary of Statistics "

tells us how the crop looks now. The
ratio of murders to each million inhabitants has stood as follows in the countries named: England, 711; Ireland, 883;
France, 796; Germany, 837; and the
United States, 2,460. Only Italy and
Spain exceed us. Do ·we wonder why
the foreigner is worse here than at
home? The answer is easy. He has
left the restraints of a watchful government; our liberty is for him license. On
the frontier he is exposed to the worst
influences, and for years has no religious
instruction nor even example. Is it
strange that death reaps such a harvest?
The sowers go forth to sow. In due
time that seed ripens to the harvest.

The *Police Gazette* is sowing dragon's
teeth most diligently. The log shanties
of the lumbermen are often papered with
them. Nice primers these for "young
America"! Sober Maine sends streams
of polluted literature out here, with cheap
chromo attachments, and the Sunday-
school lesson in them for an opiate.

The infidel lecturer is sowing his seed on the fruitful soil of runaway guilt. The callow scientist is dropping seed long since *dropped* in another way by real scientists. The whole country is sown with newspapers of all grades, and the crop is coming up. What shall the harvest be?

"Be not deceived, whatsoever a nation soweth, that shall it also reap."

In a very large number of new settlements all the above agencies are in active operation before the missionary arrives; and, oh, what a field he finds! The farmer on the new farm cannot use the drill and improved implements for the uneven places and stumps, but must needs sow by hand, and sometimes between the log piles, a little here and a little there, and then, between times, spend his strength underbrushing.

So the missionary starts without a church building, choir, organ, or even a membership, his pulpit a box in a vacant store, or in a schoolhouse or railway depot, or some rude log house of the settler; his audience is gathered from the four corners of the earth — representatives of a dozen sects, backsliders in abundance, and those who have run away from the light of civilized life. Many among the latter have broken their marriage vows, and are now living in unlawful wedlock.

I remember ·once preaching on this evil to an audience of less than twenty, and was surprised at the close of the meeting to hear a woman say, " Did you know you gave Mrs. —— an awful crack on the knuckles to-day?"

I said, " No!"

"Well, ye did, ye know."

Mentioning the circumstance with surprise to another, I received for an answer, "Well, she needn't say nothin'; she's in the same boat herself!"

Depressed in spirits, I told my troubles to a good lady who I knew was "one of the salt of the earth," and noticing a smile come over her face, I asked her what she was smiling at. She replied, " The third was as bad as the other two ! "

Just here is one of the greatest hindrances the missionary has to contend with. I am not sure but it rivals the saloon. One missionary I visited told me that in one little hamlet, on his field, there was not a single family living in lawful wedlock. It is next to impossible to do anything with the parents in such cases. But there is one bright side to this dark picture. Almost without exception, they like to have their children attend the Sabbath-school. Here is prolific soil in which to sow good seed, and we cannot commence too soon.

We are living in rushing times. I have just read in a paper that one town in Ontonagon County, one year and a half old, has three thousand inhabitants, forty-five saloons, twelve hotels, two papers, forty-eight stores, two opera houses, and an electric plant ! With villages springing up in every county, and the immense onflowing tide from foreign shores, the lone missionary on the frontier ofttimes would despair, but for the promise of the Master, the miracles of the past, and the joy of hope's bright harvest in the future. And so, "going forth weeping, bearing precious seed," he sows beside all waters, with full expectations that " He shall come again rejoicing, bringing His sheaves with Him."

That the reader may have an idea of the vastness of the field, and the distances between the workers, I will jot down a few facts. In 1887 there were thirty Congregational churches in the three conferences of Grand Traverse, Cheboygan, and Chippewa and Mackinac. These conferences had an average width of sixty miles, and stretch from Sherman, in the south of Grand Traverse Conference, for a hundred and fifty-eight miles, as the bird flies, to Sugar Island, in the north of Chippewa and Mackinac Conference.

No one can say we were crowded. My nearest neighbor was sixteen miles away, the next thirty, and the next forty; and, unless a change has come very lately, this is the only self-supporting church in the three conferences — and that because it was settled thirty years prior to many of the other churches. Ten years ago there were hundreds of miles of unbroken forests where to-day are crowded summer resorts and busy villages, filled with representatives of the most diverse nationalities under the sun. I have preached to a good-sized audience with not a single person in it that was born in the United States. And the cry is, Still they come. Now send on your harvesters!

XXIX.

" HARVEST HOME."

AFTER all the hopes and fears and toil of the summer, the farmer's most beautiful sight is to see the last great load safe in the barn, the stock fattening on the rich, sweet aftermath, the golden fruit in the orchard, and the big, red, harvest moon smiling over all. This is a frequent sight, despite poor crops and bad weather. The successful farmer does not rely on one, but a variety of crops. Then, if the season is bad for corn, it will be good for oats or wheat. Some crop will repay his labor.

Here is a hint for the home missionary who goes forth to sow spiritual seed. If he expects to get a crop of Congregationalists, he will often lament over poor returns. Often the missionary finds himself in a miscellaneous gathering, like that of Pentecost in its variety, and no mere "ism" will crystallize them. One is of Paul, another of Apollos or Cephas, and he must "determine not to know anything among them save Christ and him crucified." He must drop minor points, and adopt that plan on which all can agree.

Here is a bit of experience. In a community of seven hundred souls, the following denominations were represented: Baptists, three kinds; Presbyterians, two kinds; Methodists, four kinds; Christians, "Church of God," Episcopalians, Roman Catholics, Seventh-day Adventists, Lutherans of all branches, Quakers, and Congregationalists. One day I found three married women making ready to keep house in what had been a large store, the only vacant place in which to live; their husbands were working and living in camp. I said, "I am glad to see you. I suppose you are all Christians?"

To my surprise, they all cheerfully responded, "Yes."

"Well, that is good news," I said. "And to what church do you belong?"

" Church of God," was their answer.

" Good ; so do I. Have you brought your letters?"

" No."

" But do you really belong to the ' Church of God'?" said one. " Well, I *am* glad to think we should find a ' Church of God' minister way up here !"

This she said addressing the other women.

" Oh, well," said one, " he means that every church is a church of God!"

" Oh !" was the answer, with a shade of disappointment on her face.

" Well, well," I said, " is not that true ?"

" Y-a-as ; but it is not like ourn."

" What do you believe different from me ?"

" Well, we believe in feet-washing for one thing, and in immersion."

" Oh, well, I think Christians should wash their feet too."

" Now, Elder, that ain't right to be

making fun of Scripter; for Christ told his disciples to wash one another's feet, and said, 'Happy are ye if ye do these things.'"

I explained what I thought was the meaning of the lesson, but she shook her head.

I said, "Are you happy?"

"Not very.   I feel lonesome here."

"But is not Christ here too?"

"Oh, yes; but it is not home."

"Well, I am glad you belong to Christ, and hope you will unite with us in fighting the common foe. Will you come to church, and bring the children to our Sabbath-school?"

"Well, we shall do that."

As I was leaving one of them said, "There is a new-comer across the street. She belongs to some church *outside*." By "outside" she meant the old, settled parts. "You better call on her."

I did so, and said that I was the home missionary.   I asked her how she liked her new home?

"Not much. It is a dreadfully wicked place."

"Yes, that is true; and I hope you will lend a hand in the good work. You are a Christian, I believe?"

"Yes; but I don't belong to your church."

"What church are you now a member of?"

"Well, there is only one of my kind in the State that I know of."

"You must feel lonesome at times; but in what do you differ from us?"

"Well, we believe in being immersed three times in succession, face downwards. I intend doing what I can."

After giving her a cordial invitation to attend the church, I left the good woman, saying I hoped I could depend on her being at church. But, alas! trade became so brisk that the good sister had to work Sundays. She felt very sorry, she said, but it did seem as if it was impossible to live a Christian life in such a wicked place; and she had concluded not to give her letter to the church until she could get into a better community, where she would not have to work Sundays. I told her I was surprised that one who had been so thoroughly cleansed should have fallen away so quickly.

"Yes; but it is such a wicked place."

"I know; but you have only to be just a small Christian here to pass for a first-class saint!"

She smiled sadly, and said she guessed she would wait.

A man that must have a "New England element" to work in will feel depressed in such a field. But if, like Wesley, his field is the world, or, like Paul, he can say to the people, "called to be saints," then he can thrust in the sickle and begin harvesting. We must not only sow beside all waters, but reap too. Do not harvest the weeds and the darnel, nor reject the barley because it is not wheat. Often in the new settlements there are enough Christians to form the nucleus of one church; whereas, if we wait to have a church for each sect, it means waste of money and waste of men.

In one small town of less than three hundred people, where there were many denominations represented, the company that owned nearly all the land gave a lot and the lumber for a church. Most of the Christians united, and a minister was secured. Some, however, would not join with their brethren, but waited on the superintendent to get a lot for themselves. He said, " Yes, we will give you all a lot and help you build. Just as soon as this church becomes self-supporting we will give the next strongest a lot, and so on to the end."

This is level-headed Christian business. If we want to reap the harvest, we must " receive him that is weak in the faith." Hidden away in trunks are hundreds of church letters that should be coaxed out. Faithful preaching, teaching, and visiting, will bring a glorious " Harvest Home." A goodly sight it is to see, under one roof, all these different branches of the

Lord's army worshipping the same Master, rejoicing in the same hope, and realizing in a small degree that there is neither Jew nor Greek, bond nor free, male nor female, but that all are one in Christ Jesus.

XXX.

INJEANNY VS. HEAVEN.

THE title to this chapter bears about the same relation to its contents as the name of one sermon does to the other twenty in a given volume. I gave it this title because it must have some heading; everything has a heading. Graves have headstones.

No greater variety of character exists on the frontier than elsewhere, but peculiar cases come to the surface oftener. Those women living in the woods, who belonged to the " Church of God," are good illustrations. They had some peculiar ideas about the Scriptures, but it was much more refreshing to the missionary to find *peculiar* views than none at all. I often introduced myself to them with a text of Scripture, and tried hard to induce them to move into the next village for their children's sake. It was a much better place morally, although but a mile distant. But the influence of an organized church, with a good building and Sunday-school, made a greater difference than the distance would seem to warrant. One day, as I was passing their home, I shouted out, " Up, get you out of this place; for the Lord will destroy this city!" The next day I was off on my way to the other side of the State. As my journey well illustrates the difficulties of travel in a new country, I will describe it.

At my first change of cars, I found that my train was delayed by a fire along the track, so that I could not make my next connection with a cross-country train. This troubled me, as it was Friday, and the young minister whom I was about to visit was doing manual work on his church building, and would probably be ill-prepared to preach himself. I telegraphed him, and was just turning away when my eye caught sight of a map, and I noticed that the road I was on and the road he was on, although a hundred miles apart where I was then, gradually approached until within thirteen miles of each other, one hundred miles north. Remembering that a stage crossed at this point, I started on the late train, which, like a human being, seldom makes up for lost time, and was dropped into the pitch darkness about eleven P.M. The red lights of the train were soon lost in the black forest; I felt like Goldsmith's last man.

Two or three little lights twinkled from some log cabins. A small boy, with a dilapidated mail-bag and a dirty lantern, stood near me. I asked him if there was a hotel in town.

He said, " Yep."

Would he guide me to it?

" Yep."

I next inquired whether the stage made connections with the train on the other road.

" Wal, yes, it gineraley does."

" Why, does it not to-morrow?"

" Guess not."

"Why?"

" Cos' of the ternado."

" Tornado?"

" Yes; didn't ye know we had a ternado?"

" No."

" Well, we did, ye know; tore the trees up hullsale, and just played Ned. Rain cum down like suds."

" Well, can I get a buggy or wagon?"

" Guess not; both out in the woods; can't git home."

I felt sick at hearing this; for how to get across with two grips filled with books, theological books too, troubled me. I slept little. My room was bare; the rain pattering on the roof, the mosquitoes inside, and my own thoughts, routed me out early Saturday morning. I was pleased to find that the man had returned with the wagon, and after much persuasion, I engaged him for five dollars to take me across.

We started off with an axe. The old settlers laughed at our attempt, but we were young. Over the fallen trees we went bumping along; but, alas, we tried too big a maple, and out came the reach-pole and left us balanced on the tree. After a tiring walk through the " shin-tangles " — that is, ground hemlock — we reached the road, and mounted bareback. We met some commercial travellers cutting their way through, with a settler's help, passed a horse and buggy (minus a driver), with a bottle of whiskey in the bottom. We then had the good fortune to borrow a single wagon of a minister, who lived near on a farm. Our horses had to walk in the water by the edge of the lake, and the leeches fastened on them by the dozen. Finally we met the stage, and knew our way was clear. We were drenched with the rain, but it was clearing, and so we cheered up.

I asked the stage-driver whether I could catch the train.

He said, " Well, if ye *drive*, ye can."

The emphasis he put into the drive made us whip up. Presently the village could be seen, a half-mile away. The engine was on the turntable. How fast it went around! I was getting nervous. I asked the man to get my grips out, while I got my ticket; and rushing into the office, I snapped out, "Ticket for —— !"

The man turned his head with a jerk, and stared at me so intently that I thought something was wrong. So I said, "What time does the train start?"

"In about an hour."

You could have knocked me over with a feather. I felt like Sir Francis Drake. when his vessel seemed to be going over in the Thames. "What! have I sailed the ocean," said he, " to be drowned in a ditch?" So, I thought, "Have I come a hundred miles out of my way, to miss the train?"

I boarded the cars, cleaned my valises, and found the color running from my book-covers. My boots were like brown paper, so sodden were they. I dried myself by the stove; but my troubles were not over. The train-boy called out the station at the water-tank. The rain was pouring down; I was in for it again; so I walked down between the freight cars, went to the hotel and dried myself again, and, after dancing around the room on one foot to get my boots on, I started off to find my man.

He was out of town! Expected home with a funeral soon. I was foolish enough to make myself known as soon as he got off the cars, and he coaxed me into taking charge of the funeral. Then for the third time I was soaked, as we stood in the new cemetery, while a hymn of six verses was rendered. But what flattened me worse than all was that the young man had not received my second telegram, which I sent to relieve his supposed excited feelings, and had not been troubled in the least, but was going to make Fred. Robertson (" who being dead yet speaketh ") do duty for him. Tired out, I flung myself on a bed, and slept in spite of — well never mind what. I had to change quarters next night, for I was not so sleepy.

I received a letter from the student who had taken my charge, saying, "——— is burnt to the ground, and all north of the railway." In an instant there flashed on my mind the words of the woman: "Up, get you out," etc. The same words came home to the women as they saw their homes going up in smoke.

"What did the elder say?" said they to one another.

The excitement of the fire brought on brain fever in the case of the youngest child.

On my return, while trying to comfort the little one (who we thought was dying), and telling her about heaven, she cried out in her feebleness, "I don't want to go to heaven! I want to go to Injeanny."

And, sure enough, she got well, and did go to "Injeanny."

XXXI

THE LATEST FRONTIER — OKLAHOMA.

COLLIER, in his "Great Events of History," tells of a million warriors who, leaving their wives and children, crossed the Danube, and swore allegiance to Rome. Since that time a great many immigrations have taken place, but none on so large a scale. But, large or small, the settlements of the Indian Territory, now called Oklahoma, are the most unique.

It would have been hard to have devised a worse way to open a new country. Thousands of people — strong, weak, the poor settler, the speculator, the gambler — were all here, man and wife, and spinster on her own responsibility. All waited for weeks on the border-land. At last the time came, and the gun was fired, and in confusion wild as a Comanche raid, the great rush was made. Many sections being claimed by two and three parties, the occasion had its comic side, amid more that was tragic. Thousands went in on cattle-cars, and as many more filled common coaches inside and out, and clung to the cow-catcher of the engine. In places wire fences were on either side of the railway; and men in trying to get through them in a hurry, often reached their land minus a large part of their clothing.

In one case a portly woman, taking the tortoise plan of slow and steady, reached the best section, while the men still hung in the fence like victims of a butcher-bird. It is said of one young woman, who made the run on horseback, that reaching a town-site, her horse stumbled, and she was thrown violently to the ground and stunned. A passing man jumped off his horse, and sprinkled her face with water from his canteen; and as she revived, the first thing she said was, "This is my lot."

LOOKING FOR A TOWN LOT.

Page 294.

" No, you don't," said the man. But to settle it they went to law, and the court decided in favor of the woman, as she struck the ground first.

Among much that was brutal and barbarous, some cases of chivalry were noticed. In one case a young woman was caught in a wire fence, and two young men went back, helped her out, and allowed her to take her choice of a section. One man, in his eagerness, found himself many miles from water. As he was driving his stake, he noticed that his horse was dying; and realizing his awful situation, being nearly exhausted with thirst, he cut his horse's throat, drank the blood, and saved his own life.

The work done in six years is simply marvellous. Imagine the prairie described by Loomis as the place where you could see day after to-morrow coming up over the horizon ; at times covered with flowers fair as the garden of the Lord, or covered with snow, and nothing to break the fury of the wind. Seventy-five thousand Indians the only permanent residents in the morning ; at night hundreds of thousands of whites — villages, towns, and cities started, in some of them a mayor chosen, a board of aldermen elected, and the staked-out streets under police control. The inhabitants were under tents for a few weeks, while sickness of all kinds attacked them. There were rattlesnakes of two varieties, tarantulas, two kinds of scorpions, — one, the most dangerous, a kind of lizard, which also stings with its tail, and with often deadly effect, — and centipedes that grow to six inches in length. One of the latter was inside a shirt which came home from the laundry, and planted his many feet on the breast of one of our minute-men, and caused it to swell so fearfully that he thought at one time he should die. He recovered, but still at times feels the effect of the wounds, which are as numerous as the feet. The pain caused is intense, and the parts wounded slough off.

Now imagine all this ; and then six

years after you visit this land, and find cities of ten thousand inhabitants, banks with polished granite pillars, — polished with three per cent per month interest, — great blocks, huge elevators, and fine hotels. And nowhere, even in Paris, will you find more style than among the well-to-do. And on the same streets where I saw all this, I also saw men picking kernels of corn out of an old cellar close by a second-hand store, where already the poor had given up and sold their furniture to get home.

I looked out of my hotel window one morning in "Old Oklahoma," and saw a lady walking past dressed in a lavender suit, a white hat with great ostrich feathers on it, by her side a gentleman as well groomed as any New York swell, an English greyhound ambled by their side, while in the rear were rough men with the ugly stiff hats usually worn by your frontier rough. Storekeepers were going to work in their shirt-sleeves. This was in a town of two thousand inhabitants, where there were four banks, four newspapers, eleven churches, and only three saloons.

While I was there a most brutal murder took place, — a woman shot her step-daughter, killing her instantly. The husband, the girl's father, swept the blood from the sidewalk, and went down to the jail that night and stayed with the woman, while a fiddler was sent down to cheer her. This man was her fifth husband.

In the two weeks I was in that vicinity seven persons were killed. Three men had shot down some train-robbers, and after they were dead had filled their bodies with bullets. This so incensed the friends of the dead men that a number of them went to the house where the men had fortified themselves. When they saw how large a force was against them, they surrendered, their wives in the meanwhile begging the men who had come not to molest their husbands. But the women were pushed rudely aside, and

FORMING IN LINE TO VOTE FOR MAYOR.

the men were carried to the hills and lynched. One murderer cost the Territory over fifteen thousand dollars. Banks have loaded pistols behind the wire windows, where they can be reached at a moment's notice.

Still, lawlessness is not the rule; and it has never been as bad as one city was farther north, where men were held up on the main street in broad daylight. Such facts may just as well be known, because there is a better time coming, and these things are but transitory.

In the old settled parts, peach orchards are already bearing; and if there is a moderate rainfall, and the people can get three good crops out of five, such is the richness of the soil, the people will be rich. But to me the western part of the Territory seems like an experiment as yet. There are many places in the same latitude farther north utterly deserted; and empty court-houses, schools, and churches stand on the dry prairie as lonesome as Persepolis without her grandeur.

But now let us go into "The Strip." ("The Strip" is the Cherokee Strip, the last but one opened; the Kickapoo being opened this May.) It has been settled about eighteen months. It is May, 1895. We leave the train, and start across the prairie in a buggy with splendid horses that can be bought for less than forty dollars each. We pass beautiful little ponies that you can buy for ten to twenty dollars. On either side we pass large herds of cattle and many horses. Few houses are in sight, as most of them are very small and hardly distinguishable from the ground, while some are under ground. Here and there a little log house, made from the "black jacks" that border the stream, which is often a dry ditch. The rivers, with banks a quarter of a mile apart at flood can be stepped over to-day.

Fifty miles of riding bring us to a county town. All the county towns in "The Strip" were located by the Government, and have large squares, or rather

INDIANS AT PAWNEE, OKLAHOMA TERRITORY.

oblongs, in which the county buildings stand. It is the day before the Indians are paid. Here we find every one busy. Streets are being graded, and a fine courthouse in process of erection. Stores are doing an immense business, one reaching over one hundred thousand dollars a year; another, larger still, being built. By their sides will be a peanut-stand, a sod store, another partly of wood and partly of canvas, and every conceivable kind of building for living in or trading. And here is a house with every modern convenience, up to a set of china for afternoon teas, and a club already formed for progressive euchre.

The Indian is not a terror to the settlers, as in early days; but he exasperates him, stalking by to get his money from the Government. He spends it like a child, on anything and everything to which he takes a notion. He lives on canned goods, and feasts for a time, then fasts until the Great Fathers send him more money. On the reservation, gamblers fleece him; but he does not seem to care, for he has a regular income and all the independence of a pauper.

It seemed very strange to look out of the car window, and see the tepees of the Indians, and on the other side of the car a lady in riding-habit with a gentleman escort — a pair who would have been in their place in Rotten Row.

Now we must turn westward for a hundred miles, and in all the long ride pass but one wheatfield that will pay for cutting; and that depends on rain, and must be cut with a header. Dire distress already stares the settler in the face; and even men, made desperate by hunger in Old Oklahoma, are sending their petitions to Guthrie for food. There are hundreds of families who have nothing but flour and milk, and some who have neither. When a cry goes up for help, it is soon followed by another, saying things are not so bad. This latter cry comes from those who hold property, and who would rather the people starve than that property should decrease.

I saw men who had cut wood, and hauled it sixteen miles, then split it, and carried it twelve miles to market, and after their three days' work the two men had a load for themselves and one dollar and a quarter left. And one man said, " Mine is a case of ' root hog or die,'" and so got fifty cents for his load of wood he had brought fourteen miles; while 'another man returned with his, after vainly offering it for forty cents. In one town I saw a horse, — a poor one, it is true, — but the man could not get another bid after it had reached one dollar and a half.

Of course there are thousands who are better off; but in the case of very many they were at the very last degree of poverty when they went in. Many of our minute-men preached the first Sunday. They were among the men who sat on the cow-catcher of the engine, and made the run for a church-lot and to win souls. They preached that first Sunday in a dust-storm so bad that you could scarcely see the color of your clothes. To those who never saw one, these dust-storms are past belief. Even when the doors and windows are closed, the room seems as if it were in a fog; for the fine particles of dust defy doors and windows. And should a window be left open, you can literally use a shovel to get the dust off the beds.

You may be riding along, as I was, the hot wind coming in puffs, the swifts gliding over the prairie by your side, the heat rising visibly on the horizon, when in a flash, a dust-storm from the north came tearing along, until you could not see your pony's head at times, drifts six inches deep on the wheat, and your teeth chattering with the cold at one P.M., when at eleven A.M. you were nearly exhausted with the heat.

Strange when you ask people whether it is not extremely hot in the Middle West, they say, " Yes; but we always have cool nights." And, as a rule, that is so; but now as I write, July 9, 1895, comes the news of intense heat, — thermometer a hundred and nine in the shade, and ninety-eight at midnight, followed by a storm that shot pebbles into the very brickwork of the houses.

Every man who can, has a cyclone cellar. Some are fitted up so that you could keep house in them. In one town where I went to speak, the meeting was abandoned on account of a storm which was but moderate; but such is the fear of the twister that nearly all the people were in their pits.

In the Baptist church, where they had a full house the night before, I found one woman and two men; and they were blowing out the lights. The telegrams kept coming, telling of a storm shaking buildings, and travelling forty miles an hour; but it was dissipated before it reached me, and I escaped. Yet I found a man who had lived over a quarter of a century in the West, and had never seen one.

It is a big country. A friend of mine in England wrote me that they feared for me as they read of our fearful cyclones.

I was living near Boston, Mass. I wrote back, saying I felt bad for them in London when the Danube overflowed. I had to go over and explain it before they saw my joke.

The cyclone, however, is no joke. Nevertheless, it performs some queer. antics. One cyclone struck a house, and left nothing but the floor and a tin cuspidore. The latter stood by a stove which weighed several hundredweight, and which was smashed to atoms.

In another house a heavy table was torn to pieces, while the piano-cover in the same room was left on the piano. In one house all had gone into the cellar, when they remembered the sleeping baby. A young girl sprang in, and got the baby; and just as she stepped off, the house went, and she floated into the cellar like a piece of thistle-down. A school-teacher was leaving school, when she was thrown to the ground, and every bit of clothing was stripped from her, leaving her without a scratch.

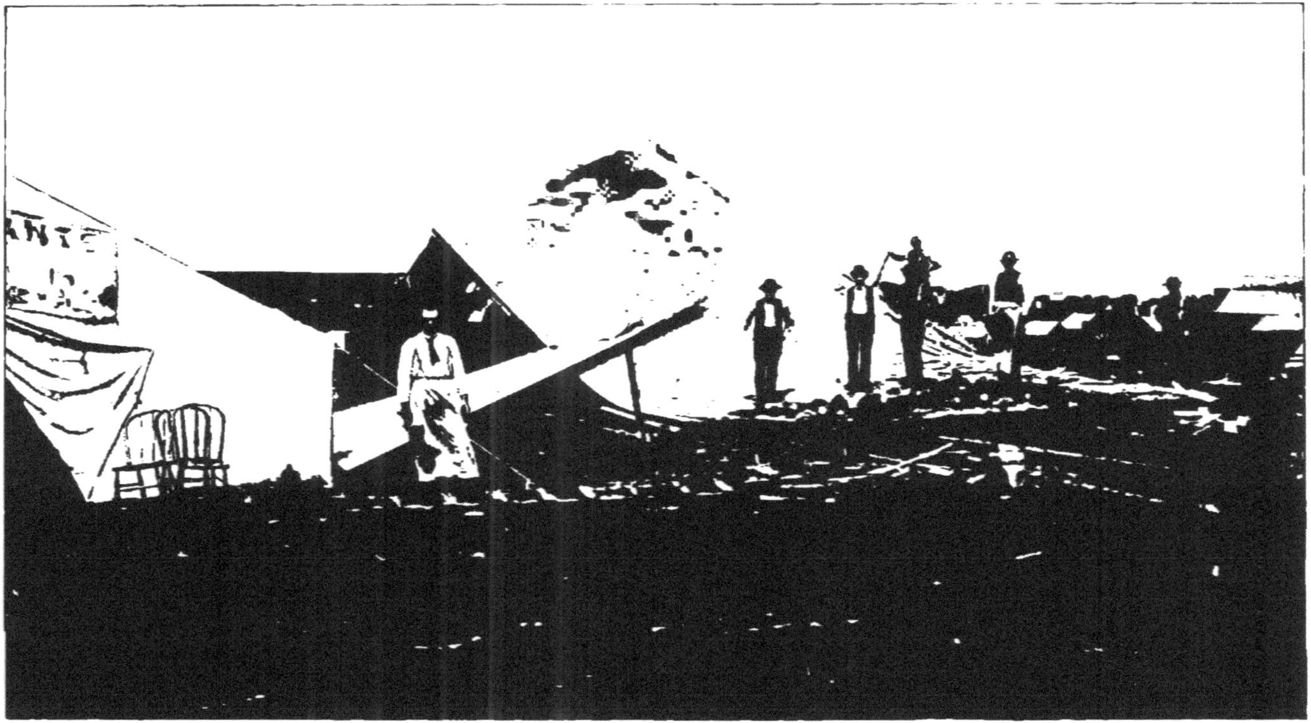

AFTER A STORM, GUTHRIE, OKLAHOMA TERRITORY.

Perhaps the most remarkable escape was a few years ago in Kansas City. When a young school-teacher reached home, her mother said, " Why did you not bring your young brother ? " She hastened back ; and as she reached the room where her brother was, she grasped him around the waist, and jumped out of the window just as the building was struck. She was carried two blocks, and dropped without injury to either of them. These things are hard to believe, but no one will be lost who does not believe them.

But to return to our journey. We had three churches to dedicate in three days, two on one day. And here let me say, a church could be organized every day in the year, and not trespass on any one's work. We could see the little building loom up on the horizon, appearing twice its size, as things do on the prairie with nothing to contrast them with, for the houses were almost invisible. The place was crowded, so that the wagon-seats were brought in ; and a very affecting sight it was to see the communion-wine brought in a ketchup bottle. The people were good, but very poor, although nearly all owned horses, for in that country this is no sign of wealth.

After a few hours' drive, we came to our second church. The prairie here was broken up by small cañons, interspersed with streams, and was quite pretty. A grocery and a blacksmith-shop, the latter opened Tuesday and Thursday only, comprised the village. A small house where the proprietor of the store lived, and the church, were all the buildings one could see. The people were very cordial and intelligent. The daughters of mine host were smart, handsome girls, that could do almost everything, — ride a wild broncho, and shoot a rattler's head off with a bullet, and yet were modest, well-dressed, and good-mannered young ladies.

I was taken down stairs cut out of the clay, and covered with carpet, into a room the sides of which were the cañon. It looked out over the great expanse. The

FIRST CHURCH AND PARSONAGE, ALVA, OKLAHOMA TERRITORY.

Page 307.

beds were lifted up so as to form walls around the room, and take up less space.

After a bountiful supper, I looked at the church, which stood on a sightly hill. I wondered where the people were coming from, but was told it would be filled. It was on a Thursday night. I looked over the prairie; and in all directions I saw dark spots in motion, that grew larger. I said, " They appear as if rising from the ground."

" Well," said mine host, " most of them are."

By eight o'clock three hundred were there, most of them bringing chairs; by 8.30, there were four hundred; at 9 o'clock, by actual count, five hundred people crowded in and around the door of the church. It was a sight never to be forgotten, to see this great company start off across the prairie in the full moonlight. I spoke to some of them, saying," Why, you were out at the afternoon meeting." — " Yes," said the man, " I should have come if we had to ride a cow all the way from Enid." This was a place thirty miles away. This church was built by the people, one man working for a dollar a week and his dinner, the farmers working his farm for him while he was at the building.

The church had not yet received its chairs, and was seated with boards laid across nail-kegs.

Here our minute-man preaches in houses so small that the chairs had to be put outside, and the people packed so thickly that they touched him. It ought to touch the Christian reader to help more. We had fifty miles to ride the next day, into a county town. We found it all alive; for nearly four hundred lawsuits were on the docket, mostly for timber stealing.

"Poor fellows," I thought, "Uncle Sam ought to give you the timber for coaxing you here."

However, the judge was a fine, well-read man, and let them off easy. Deputy-sheriffs by the score were stalking about,

AT A CHURCH DEDICATION.

Page 300.

with their deadly revolvers sticking out
from under their short coats.

The best hotel was crowded, and I had
for that night to sleep in another one.
The house was old, and had been taken
down and brought here from Kansas and
rebuilt. The doors up-stairs once had
glass in them; rough boards covered the
broken places. One door was made up
entirely of old sign-boards, which made
it appear like so many Chinese characters, such as Pat said he could not read,
but thought he could play it if he had
his flute with him.

I was ushered into a room, and requested to put the light out when I was
through with it; meaning I was to place it
outside, which I did not do. But what
a room! The wainscoting did not reach
the floor. Small bottles of oil, with
feathers in them, looked awfully supicious.
There was no washstand or water. The
pillow looked like a little bag of shot,
and was as dirty as the bed-clothes. The
door was fastened with a little wooden

button, which hung precariously on a small nail.

I took off my coat, and put it on again, and finally lay down on the bed, after placing something between my head and that pillow.

I had to go several blocks in the morning to find a place to wash, so dirty were the towels down-stairs. I was then given a house to myself, which consisted of a single room, eight by ten, or ten by twelve, I forget which. It was originally the church and parsonage. Here the church was organized, and the first wedding took place.

A fine church, the largest and handsomest in the Territory, was next door, and was to be dedicated the next day, which would be Sunday. This building had been brought all the way from Kansas, and the very foundation-stones carried with it, and put up in better shape than ever. Three times next day it was crowded, even to the steps outside, many coming twenty miles to attend. One lady came twice who lived six miles away, and said, "Oh, how I wish I could come again to-night! But I have six cows to milk, and it would mean twelve miles to ride there and back, and then six miles to go home; yet I would if I could. Oh! sometimes I think I should die but for God and my little girl."

As the people came in, I said to myself, "Where have I seen these ladies before, — pink and lemon-colored silk dresses, pointed buff shoes, ostrich feathers in their enormous hats, — oh! I have it, in the daily hints from Paris."

The men wore collars as ugly and uncomfortable as they could be made, which made them keep their chins up; and right by their sides were women whose hats looked like those we see in boxes outside the stores, your choice for five cents; there were four or five little sunburned children, some of whom were in undress uniform, and their fathers in homespun and blue jeans.

Close by in the cañons crouched a fugitive from justice. Two men started out to take him, but came home without their guns. Then a brave, cool-headed man of experience went, and slept in the timber where our desperado lay concealed, thinking to catch him in the morning before the robber awoke ; but while he was rubbing his own sleepy eyes the words, sharp as a rifle report, came, " Hold up your hands!" And number three came home minus his shooting-irons.

Oklahoma differs in many ways from other frontiers. You find greater extremes, but you also find a higher type intellectually. The *Century* and *Harper's* and the popular magazines sell faster, and more of them, than the *Police Gazette*.

On the other hand, settled *en masse* as it has been, the church has not begun to reach the people except in county towns, where, as usual, it is too often, but not always, overdone. In one case I found a man who was trying to organize with one member ; and in another a man actually built a church before a single member of his denomination was there, and there were none there when I left. In some cases I found our minute-man an old soldier; and more than once for weeks at a time he had to sleep in his clothes, and keep his rifle by his side.

In some cases the Government had located a county town, and the railway company had chosen another site close by. Then the fight began. The railway at first ignored the Government's site, and ran their trains by; built a station on their own site, and would have no other. Then the people on the Government site tore up the tracks, and incendiarism became so common that the insurance agent came and cancelled all the policies except the church and parsonage where our minute-man stood guard. This was done in several places, and the end is not yet.

Now, to the general reader, everything seems in a hopeless muddle, and he is glad he is not living there. But remember this. It is better than some older settlements, where men had to give eighty bushels of wheat for a pair of stogy boots, as they did in Ohio, and fight the Indian as well as the wolf from the door, or in Kansas forty years ago, where corn brought five cents a bushel, and men had to go a hundred miles to the mill. In order to show the hopeful side, I will give an illustration.

I was to speak at a meeting in Illinois. My way was through Missouri, where spiritual and civilized prosperity has not kept pace with her wealth and opportunities. I was entertained in a mansion built sixty years ago. The city, of sixteen thousand inhabitants, could hardly be matched in New England, — many fine streets, shaded with grand old elms; the roads bricked and well graded; the houses beautiful, artistic, and surrounded with lovely lawns; a college, a ladies' seminary, and many fine schools and churches.

The lady of the house said, "My mother crossed the mountains many times to Washington, to live with her husband, who represented the State there." At

last she had to take two carriages and two
horses, and it became too hard work,
when her husband built the house which
is still a beautiful home, with magnificent
elms, planted by its original owner, shad-
ing it.   In that day the rattlesnake glided
about the doorway, the Indians roamed
everywhere, and the wolves actually licked
the frosting off the cakes that were set to
cool on the doorstep, while the Indians
stole the poor woman's dinner who lived
close by.   To-day a park adorns the front,
given by the generous owner to the city;
and where the wolves and the Indians
roamed, lives the daughter of Governor
Duncan, with her husband and family, in
one of the finest cities of its size in the
world.   Nowhere in all this wide world
can the advance of civilization during the
last fifty years be found on so large a
scale as here on the American frontiers.

XXXII.

THE PIONEER WEDDING.

As one travels over our country to-day, one will see as lowly homes, as acute poverty, and as congested a population, as he can find anywhere in Europe, with this great difference, — our people are filled with hope. There is a buoyancy about American life that is lacking in Europe. It is, as Emerson expressed it, a land of opportunity; and this difference is everything to the immigrant and the native pioneer. And this means much to us. The great majority of immigrants are from the most thrifty of the poor.

I have in mind now a family, who once lived in a large city. It took all the strength of husband and wife to make both ends meet; but by dint of rigid economy, they saved enough to take them across the water in the steerage of a great ship. This couple, with their little ones, found themselves at the end of their journey on a homestead, but with scarcely a cent left. The people around them were very poor, some of them living the first winter on potatoes and salt, not having either bread or milk. But in some way they managed to live, cheered by the hope that any move must be upward, and in the near future comfort, and farther on affluence. The same economy that saved the passage-money kept a little for a rainy day, no matter how hard the times were.

When I became acquainted with them they owned a large farm, a small log house and stable, several cows, horses, pigs, and poultry. Around the house was a neat picket-fence, every picket being cut out and made with axe and jack-knife during the long winter months. The vegetable garden was well-stocked; but what appealed to me most was the richness and the variety of the flower-garden, — roses, pansies, wallflowers, sweet-pease, hollyhocks, and mignonette. It was truly a feast for the eyes. The little house and the milk-room, the latter made of lilliputian logs, were dazzling white by the repeated coats of whitewash. The whole formed a pretty picture; and for so new a country it was more than a picture, — it was an education for every settler near them.

I tried to fancy my host's feelings as he thought of the sharp struggle in the old land, and as he looked over his broad acres now, richer than the farmers he once envied as they drove in on their stout cobs to market.

Near by was another home. Here, too, were fine gardens, and another old couple out of the grip of poverty, which well-nigh killed them in the struggle. This good lady was once the only white woman on a large island, which to-day is laid out in sections, has towns, villages, schoolhouses, and churches, and every farm occupied. The old couple had an unmarried son left; and he, too, was about to quit the parent nest, and start a home for himself. And now I must tell about the wedding.

But first a word about the climate, soil, and conditions, in order to understand what follows. The whole country had once been forest, the home of the Hurons, Chippewas, and other tribes of Indians. The Jesuit had roamed here, suffered, and often become a martyr. Some time in the past, either from Indian fires or carelessness, the forest caught fire, and tens of thousands of acres of choice maples and birch were burnt down to the very roots. The soil is clay, but so charged with lime that you can plough while the water follows the horses in the furrows in rivulets that dash against their fetlocks. This in clay, as a rule, would mean utter ruin until frost came, and the ground thawed again. But not so here. As the ground becomes dry, it pulverizes easily under the harrow.

This section was subject to storms that filled the narrow streams until they became dangerous torrents, sweeping all before them, and sometimes making a jam of logs twenty miles long. One spring I noticed that all the bridges were new, and that they had all been built some four feet higher than before. I was told that the spring freshets had swept everything before them, and had been so unusually high that the change of level became necessary.

It was the night before the wedding, and I was preaching in a little schoolhouse that held about twenty people. It was a very hot night for that latitude, and every one was depressed with the heat. A great black cloud covered the heavens, except an ugly streak of dirty yellow in the west. It was not long before the yellow glare was swallowed up by the night; and then from out of the dense black canopy shot streaks of vivid lightning, forked, chained, and of every variety, and "long and loud the thunder bellowed."

We were not long in closing that meeting. All that rode in our wagon had more than two miles to go. The horses were terrified, but to those who enjoy a thunder-storm it was sublime. We crossed one bridge in the nick of time; for it went thundering down as the back wheel bumped against the road, only just clear of it.

One man was asleep in his shanty, and did not know of the storm until his little dog, tired of swimming around the room, climbed on the bed, and licked his face. The man awoke, and put his hand out of the clothes and felt the water. He sprang up and lit a lamp, and found two feet of water in his room. In the morning it had run off and taken all the bridges again.

And this was the wedding morn. The bridegroom had been away for the ring, but had not returned. We were getting anxious for him when we saw two horses coming on the jump, and a wagon that was as often off the ground as on it, as it thumped along the macadamized road of a new country, with stones as large as a cocoanut, five and six feet apart; but, as the settlers said, it was good to what it once was, and I believed it too.

He came in splashed with mud; but although he had been without sleep, victorious love shone in those light blue eyes, and with his fair complexion and rich rosy cheeks he was the personification of a Viking after victory. He had covered four times the distance on account of bridges carried away.

A hasty breakfast, and off we started, forgetting, until we were almost there, the bridge which had gone down the night before. We turned back to find another bridge afloat and in pieces; but, luckily, the stream had become shallow, and after the horses had danced a cotillon, we succeeded in getting across.

As we came to the farm where the fair young bride was waiting, we found the fields under water nearly to the house. I hardly knew how we should reach it. But the bridegroom and the horses had been there before; and, as the water was only a few inches deep, we were soon at the house. The youngsters were all in great spirits. This was the first wedding in the family; and I remember how awestruck the children seemed when the bride came out, looking queenly in her white robes, but soon recovered themselves as they recognized their own sister.

The wedding over, then came the dinner. Who would have thought, as they passed that farm, of the world of happiness in that little log house? And the dinner, — a huge sirloin, which made us sing, "Oh, the roast beef of old England!" Precious little had these people had in old England; but now, besides the mighty sirloin, there were capons, ducks, lamb and green pease, mint sauce, delicious wild strawberries, damson pie, and raspberry-wine vinegar for drink.

Thank God for the possibilities of our glorious land to those who are frugal and industrious.

After dinner we sang "The Mistletoe Bough," "To the West, to the West," "Far, far, upon the Sea," "Home, Sweet Home," and "America," the youngsters singing "My Country, 'Tis of Thee," and some of the old ones " God save the Queen," to the same tune.

The young couple had the only spare room in the house, and the rest of us went up-stairs into a room that was the size of the house. There father and mother hung a sheet up, and went to bed. Some grain-sacks made the next partition; and a young student and myself took the next bed. Golden seed-corn hung over my head from the rafters; oats, pease, and wheat were in bins on either side of the bed.

To-day that one family has become many families. The old people go to church in a covered buggy. The youngest are on the home farm, and live with the parents, and lovingly tend those two brave hearts who now sit content in their golden age, waiting for the call to that better land, where the Elder Brother has prepared a mansion for them and a marriage supper, with everlasting joy.